Love is
a time of enchantment:
in it all days are fair and all fields
green. Youth is blest by it,
old age made benign:
the eyes of love see
roses blooming in December,
and sunshine through rain. Verily
is the time of true-love
a time of enchantment — and
Oh! how eager is woman
to be bewitched!

C0000 001 538 597

THE RAINBOW GLASS

The old house named Cool-na-Grena stood by the Atlantic. There was a waterfall high up, and through the spray you might see into the land of the Rainbow Glass. But there was a haunting of Cool-na-Grena — a door that opened without the touch of a hand, a room that expected the return of a dead man. Lalage came to the house to await the birth of her child. She was running away from unhappiness, as was the dark man who had come there before her.

Books by Alice Dwyer-Joyce
in the Ulverscroft Large Print Series:

THE MOONLIT WAY
THE DIAMOND CAGE
THE GINGERBREAD HOUSE
THE BANSHEE TIDE
FOR I HAVE LIVED TODAY
THE STROLLING PLAYERS
PRESCRIPTION FOR MELISSA
DANNY BOY
THE GLITTER-DUST
DOCTOR ROSS OF HARTON
THE STORM OF WRATH
THE PENNY BOX

ALICE DWYER-JOYCE

THE RAINBOW GLASS

Complete and Unabridged

ULVERSCROFT
Leicester

First published in Great Britain in 1973 by
Robert Hale Limited
London

First Large Print Edition
published July 1995
by arrangement with
Robert Hale Limited
London

British Library CIP Data

Dwyer-Joyce, Alice
The rainbow glass.—Large print ed.—
Ulverscroft large print series: romance
I. Title
823.914 [F]

ISBN 0–7089–3327–0

Published by
F. A. Thorpe (Publishing) Ltd.
Anstey, Leicestershire

Set by Words & Graphics Ltd.
Anstey, Leicestershire
Printed and bound in Great Britain by
T. J. Press (Padstow) Ltd., Padstow, Cornwall

This book is printed on acid-free paper

Prologue

IT was a July day, but except for the leaves on the trees, it might have been December . . . one of those days, when away in the back of the mind comes the thought that perhaps the end of the world is drawing near. Darker it grew and still darker and there was a wind blowing in from the sea, with a cutting edge to it. The man pulled the collar of his navy blue gaberdine coat up about his ears and shivered at the cold, comfortless loneliness of the narrow country road, that wound on, mile after empty twisting mile. As he came to the entrance of Cool-na-Grena, the sky was completely overcast by the black clouds, that raced across its expanse. The stone pillars were derelict and the wrought iron gates sagged hopelessly down from them. He peered through the gates at the overgrown avenue, creeping away out of his sight around the little grassy hill. At least there will be a house there, he thought, and shelter from this infernal wind. He lifted the gate open a little and squeezed through. Then he stepped out briskly along the drive. It twisted and coiled and turned and the trees came down to make a cold, dark tunnel, which shut out what light there was left of the day. For perhaps a quarter of a mile, the avenue snaked out before his feet. Then suddenly, he came out on a flat plateau, looking down over the stormy sea.

The house was on his right . . . a square, unimaginative house, with a flight of uneven stone steps, leading up to the front door. The roof was tiled, but several tiles were missing and the guttering was gone in places and still lay on the ground below, exactly where it had fallen. The jackdaws had built their nests in the chimneys and their raucous voices protested at the presence of a stranger, as he looked up at them. It was a big house, with two windows at either side of the front door and five across the upper storey. That much he saw at a glance. Then he realised that the dilapidation was general. The front drive must have been cared for at one time, but it had been turned into a gravelly field by the invasion of the grass. Some of the window panes had been broken and repaired with ply-wood. Even the front steps were overgrown with moss and long tufts of grass.

So this was Cool-na-Grena, he thought, 'a corner in the sun'. The name made you think that it was a place you might seek out, when the cold of the winter had gone over . . . a place where you could drowse and be happy again, but it did not resemble its name today. It was gaunt and lonely and stark and haunted. He sighed as he turned his eyes away from it and looked out to sea. The white horses of Mannanan MacLir, the Sea God, were riding the waves, and two miles off shore, a trawler was pitching and rolling on the Atlantic swell. He looked at her with the eye of an expert and knew how it would be to walk the decks and feel her moving under his feet, her timbers groaning in protest and the salt wind whistling through the rigging.

He turned back to the house and walked slowly up the steps till he came to the heavy teak front door. His hand went out to caress the wood and he thought it was like the wood of an old ship. The knocker was fashioned in the shape of a dolphin and it was almost certainly made of brass, but it was green with the neglect of years. Once more he turned to survey the view that stretched before him. The grass sloped gradually out to a little point and then the land dropped sharply to the sea. There was a hill on either side of the house, and it was as if the land had divided to let the house come to the sea in this beautiful valley. There must be a river or a stream somewhere close, for he could hear it, and then he saw it, not a hundred yards away, cascading down from the mountains at the back, coming down in small rushes and leaps and pauses, on its way to the ocean.

He went slowly down the steps and round the side of the house to the back door. He was 'back-door company' now, he thought ruefully, running his hand over his bearded chin . . . an ugly customer to meet in such a lonely place on such a dark evening. There was a girl in the yard, feeding the fowl with corn. She was wearing an old tweed skirt with a bedraggled hem and her woollen jumper was pulled down ungracefully over sturdy hips. Her hair was wisped up on the top of her head and strands of it blew untidily about her face.

"Good evening!" he said and she spun round with a start and dropped the bowl of corn. The hens rushed squawking away momentarily and then ran back again, scrambling over each other in the eagerness of their hunger and treading the corn into the ground.

"You gave me a terrible fright," she said. "What do you want?"

"I was looking for Mr Dermot Kingston."

"He's down beyond at the shore, making fast the old boat. He'll be in to his tea in half an hour. What do you want him for? If it's work you're after, there's none here. At least, there's work in plenty and no money to pay for it, so it wouldn't interest the likes of you."

"Mr Kingston will be glad to see me. He's a friend of mine."

"Well, you're welcome to come in and wait for him," the girl said doubtfully. "There's a fire in the kitchen and I daresay you're cold. You can sit down and have a cup of tea. I was just going to wet it anyway."

He took off his coat in the kitchen and she looked at his seaman's trousers and at the blue and white speckled jersey, that came up round his ears in a high, thick collar. He was very dark, his beard as black as a crow, his eyes like sloes.

"My name is Mary Bridget," remarked the girl. "What's yours?"

"You wouldn't know it."

"Are you a friend of Mr Dermot's from the war?"

He nodded his head and she looked at him doubtfully again.

"Maybe I should put you beyond in the parlour, but I only put a match to the fire, before I went out to feed the hens. It won't have had time to draw up yet and it's like winter today with the cold. You're better off where you are."

"I'm fine thanks."

She poured out tea for him from a big brown pot, that stood on the kitchen range and the tea was as brown as the water in a bog-hole, the cup chipped at the rim and thick.

"Do you take sugar?"

She paused for a moment and added ". . . Sir."

"No sugar, thank you."

She decided that he was not an Irishman. He had an accent, like you'd hear on the English wireless, or at the pictures. She should have shown him into the parlour straight off, fire or no fire. She decided that she would not sit down now and she stood there uncertainly with her hands clasped in front of her.

"Would you care for a bit of soda bread and jam? The jam is our own make, from the gooseberries in the garden. Hannah made it herself."

"And who is Hannah?"

"She's the house-keeper. She's in the town today, doing the messages, but she'll be back in time to get the supper. Wouldn't you like a bit of the soda bread?"

"No, thank you, but don't let me disturb you. Sit down and get on with your own tea."

He had noticed her worry about his social standing and he smiled at her to try to put her at her ease.

"I'd better not . . . "

Again she paused and added, " . . . Sir," as she looked at him with an anxious frown.

"Mr Dermot'll be in in a minute. Maybe he'll kill me for not putting you in the parlour."

He drank the hot, strong tea and watched her over the edge of the cup.

"That would be a bit drastic, surely? Besides, it's very pleasant here by the stove."

"There's Mr Dermot now, sir."

She snatched the cup out of his hands and pulled him up out of the kitchen chair and the next moment, Dermot Kingston was in the room, halting in his tracks, when he saw his visitor.

"Glory be to God!" he cried. "Will you look who's here, Mary Bridget?"

He strode across the room to take the other man by the shoulders.

"Look at the beard he's grown since I saw him. What did you want to do that for, in the name of God? Is it trying to disguise yourself you are? Come on through to the sitting-room and tell me all the news."

He glanced back at Mary Bridget over his shoulder.

"Go on up above and put a hot jar in the bed. No, wait a minute. Bring us in a drink, first of all, and when Hannah comes back, tell her we have a guest . . . a very welcome and honoured guest. Come on! Come on, girl! Don't stand there gawking at him. Have you never seen a man in a beard before? Bring in the whiskey and a couple of glasses and look sharp about it."

The fire in the sitting-room was burning up brightly, but the dilapidation of the outside of the house was reflected here. The carpet was threadbare and there was a hole burnt in the hearth-rug, eight inches across. The lace curtains looked moth-eaten. The heavy velvet drapes, that hung down from thick wooden poles, were dusty and faded. Mary Bridget had followed them in from the kitchen with a bottle of whiskey and two cut-glass goblets with high stems, a siphon of soda too, on a rusty tray. She put it down on the table and ran out of the room and Dermot frowned after her.

"I suppose we're lucky there's a bottle

of malt left in the house," he sighed. "The place is gone to hell."

He stretched his arms out to include the room and the house and the whole estate.

"This is the way I found it, when I got back from the war and I've done nothing to stop the rot. All I've managed to do is get deeper into debt . . . deeper and deeper, God help me!"

"But it was such a lovely place. You were never done talking about it. What went wrong?"

Dermot splashed the whiskey into the glasses and frowned across at him.

"You've heard about putting all your eggs in the one basket? My father, God rest him, did just that . . . made an idol out of my mother. She was his whole reason for living and when she died, he had no heart left for anything. He took to drinking to ease the loneliness, as many a man has done before him . . . didn't care for Cool-na-Grena any more, with her gone from it. God! When I think of the old days and the way it used to be, with horses in the stables and the whole place as smart as paint . . . "

He passed a drink to his friend and took a long pull at his own glass.

"I tried to get it on its feet again, but I've no son to come after me now . . . nor will have. I began to wonder who I was getting it ready for. You know how it is with me. There's nobody left, but a cousin of mine, beyond in London, a stocks and shares merchant . . . a man with money. He'll get it when I'm gone and he'll come over and look at it. Perhaps he'll not even bother to do that. It'll be under the hammer to the highest bidder and there'll be an end to the O'Connell Kingstons of Cool-na-Grena . . . "

It had started to rain again and the water was being driven by the force of the wind to tap against the window panes. It ran down them in streams of tears, while the fire crackled and hissed and spluttered in the grate.

"Thank God the jackdaws have left this chimney alone. They're a bloody pest and the whole place is a mill-stone about my neck. I can't put my hand to a thing, but it goes wrong on me. The mooring post of the boat is smashed now. That's the next job to see to . . . ”

He drained his glass and went back to the tray to pour himself another drink.

“But that’s enough of this gloomy talk. Let’s get on to something more cheerful. Tell me about your career in the Merchant Navy. I suppose at the rate you were going, when I last saw you, you own the whole blasted Company by now?”

The other man sighed and looked down at the amber of the whiskey in his hand.

“I haven’t been particularly successful either, Kingston. I suppose you’ve heard?”

“I hear nothing in this God-forsaken place, man. Even the wireless is broken these six months. I keep meaning to get it fixed, but I haven’t got round to it yet.”

The stranger went over to one of the windows and stood with his back to the room, looking down on the stormy sea, his voice so low, as to be almost inaudible.

“I want a bolt hole. I’ve got to disappear, if you like to put it like that. As they say in the melodramas, I want to hide my shame."

"Don't talk about shame to me . . . not you, Frazer . . . not the man, who risked his neck a dozen times in the war . . . not the man, who was one of the greatest heroes of them all!"

Frazer turned back to the fire and the steam from his wet clothes smoked out a little.

"It's a long story. It'll keep," he said wearily.

"And in the meantime, you'll get your death of cold in those clothes. What sort of a host am I at all? Come upstairs and I'll fit you out with some of my gear. We're much of a size. We'll have that beard off you too, while we're at it. It's funny how that's changed you. Remember how they used to call us Castor and Pollux? Those were the days, God be with them. Those were the days. There's times, when I'm sorry they're over and done with."

They went up the shabby staircase side by side. The paper was peeling from the walls and the smell of damp was everywhere. The balustrade was flaking white paint down on the rotten carpet and there was a patch of wet, where the rain had come through the roof. Somebody had put a bucket under it and the drops splashed with a metallic note into the water already there.

"The bloody roof will come in on me one of these days," Dermot said moodily. "I've told the contractor about it . . . asked him to see to it, but he takes no notice of me. I might as well be talking to the wall. He's too damned polite to tell me he'd come, if I paid him the money I owe him."

He put his head over the banisters and called out to Mary Bridget, who had come out to the hall below.

"Bring us up a jug of hot water and while you're at it, get us the scissors out of Hannah's work-basket."

He went into the big front bedroom and threw open the doors of the mahogany wardrobe.

"Help yourself to anything you want. What's mine is yours and always will be. Small wonder at it!"

Half an hour later, they stood side by side, before the glowing turf fire in the sitting-room, listening to the wind, that howled round the house like a banshee and rattled at the window-frames.

"There's an idea I have in my head," Dermot said slowly. "I wonder if you'd do me a good turn. It's the way you talked about Cool-na-Grena upstairs . . . and you're an old friend. You'd help me if it was in your power . . . "

He picked up his pipe and began to fill it.

"I think I'll ask you for a promise, Frazer, a promise that you'll do as I ask, before I ask it."

"That's what's called 'buying a pig in a poke', Lieutenant. It might turn out to be a chancy business."

There was a spatter of rain against the windows and a crash outside, as a loosened tile fell into the front drive.

"You'd better give me that promise before it's too late, man. The house is falling about our ears this minute. By God! I'll not see it go, not rotting away, piece by piece, and stinking of must and damp and decay. Sooner than that, I'd take a can of petrol out there into the hall . . . pile up the furniture into a bonfire . . . perch myself up on top of it and go out in a blaze of glory."

"So you want me to help you set the house on fire?" Frazer smiled.

Dermot sucked at his pipe and the flame of the struck match glowed against his face in the gloom.

"It's quite the opposite thing, as a matter of fact. We might get away with it, you and I. Have you ever noticed the crest on this ring of mine . . . the phoenix, that rises from the flames . . . and the family motto written underneath it? But you'll promise that you'll play along with me before I say another word, and that's final. And remember you told me you wanted a bolt-hole. You'd have a bolt-hole here, where you'd not be found in a million years, if you'd give me your word to throw in your hand along with mine . . ."

* * *

The storm was more boisterous as they sat over supper later on in the evening.

"We'll have to go down to see to the boat as soon as we're finished eating," Dermot remarked. "I fixed it this afternoon, but I wasn't reckoning with this mind. We're due for a thunderstorm too by the look of that sky. Christ! Wouldn't you think all hell was going to be let loose?"

Although it was dark outside, the curtains were still drawn back. The orchestra of the elements was rising to a crescendo outside the walls of the old house and every now and again, the thunder growled its bass note in the distance. The lightning had already started to flicker a warning on the horizon, as Dermot lifted his glass in a toast.

"Here's to the success of the companions in adversity . . . and to the rebirth of the phoenix. 'Resurgam!' By God! 'Resurgam!' Let's do our best to see that it does . . . "

1

The Unexpected Inheritance

I STOOD in the bathroom of our flat and tried to hide the fact that I had morning sickness. I was worried how Gareth might react to the news. He was almost certain to disapprove. After a while, I started to brush my teeth but that made me feel ill again, so I washed the toothbrush and put it in the chromium slot. Then I spread paste along the bristles of Gareth's brush. It was one of our jokes that I must perform this small service for him twice a day. It was the duty of a good wife, he said and was the real meaning of the verb 'to cherish'.

I turned to go back to the bedroom and he was standing behind me, watching me.

"I thought there was something wrong with you. You were off colour yesterday morning too."

"I think I'm going to have a baby."

"Have you seen Price?"

"I phoned him yesterday, but he says it's too early to know by an examination. He's doing a test. I didn't like to say anything till I was sure."

"Well that's a fine bit of news to spring on a man at this time of the day."

"I'm sorry," I apologised. "I don't know how it happened."

"I do," he grinned at me suddenly and I mumbled that I had thought he might be angry. After all, it was a bomb to my social life. He kissed me then and stroked my hair back from my face.

"Social life isn't important. Just think of a son. It's one's hope of eternity in a way. Suppose there's nothing after death? Suppose Christianity is one big confidence trick? Now I'll have somebody to inherit my watch and my ring and my cigarette case . . . "

In the bedroom, he paced the carpet, to and fro, making plans in his executive board-meeting style.

"I'll get Price to call and check you over. He must have something for that sickness. He'll take you into the Wimpole for the confinement of course. First babies are tricky."

I told him that was only for the expectant father but he would not laugh, but went on making plans. The baby was due in February, I told him. Then he had a holiday planned as soon as I was out of the Wimpole and he and I were to go abroad and lie in the sun all day. He had always cocooned me in cotton wool in the three years of our marriage, had surrounded me with warmth and kindness and protected me from every harshness of life . . .

Of course, I did not allow him to bring Dr Price out to visit me. A few days later, I went by appointment to call on the great man. Margaret took me through to the waiting room, where as a school-girl, I had waited to see him after my parents' death. He had advised a holiday then. I was leaving school at the end of term anyway. I had gone up to the Hebrides and there I had met Gareth and married him the following year.

I had thought 'Gareth' an unusual name. His family came from the south of Ireland and he had a cousin, who still lived there, in a house with a stranger name. I could never remember the Gaelic of it, but only the meaning. Translated it meant a 'corner in the sun'. Gareth's grandfather had lived there and his great-grandfather and so on back for generations, not that Gareth ever showed the slightest interest in it. He spoke very rarely of family matters.

I picked up the paper from the table in Dr Price's room and went to the window seat to look at the crossword. There was no concentrating on it, so I scanned the Births, Marriages and Deaths column and a paragraph leaped out at me.

> KINGSTON. At his residence, Cool-na-Grena, Ballyboy, Co. Cork, Ireland, suddenly, as the result of an accident, Dermot O'Connell Kingston, only surviving son of the late Gavin O'Connell Kingston . . .

Gareth's grandfather had been Gavin. Dermot was the Irish cousin. There was a bluebottle buzzing against the window pane at my back and I wondered if I should let him go free. The window looked as if it had not been opened for years. I forced my attention back to the notice.

Cool-na-grain-ya. That was how it was pronounced. The sound of it came back to me from somewhere. Cool-na-grain-ya . . . Then Margaret was at the door beckoning me to come and soon I was shaking hands with Dr Price.

"My dear Lalage! This is excellent . . . "

The consultation proceeded in a dignified unhurried manner, as if the rush and race of the modern day had swirled past this quiet house and left it in a backwater. Dr Price's examination was as slow and pompous and painstaking as his own manner of speaking, but at last he was finished with it.

"Dress up now and come and talk to me. I'll telephone the Wimpole and arrange for your room."

His plummy voice spoke to the matron and discussed dates and rooms and nurses and by the time he was done, I was dressed and sitting opposite his desk on a Chippendale chair with a red leather seat. Then Margaret put her head round the door and I thought she looked rather flustered.

"There's an urgent call on my phone, Doctor. Would you like to take it in my office?"

He looked at her irritably over his glasses and tut-tutted at her that she should know he was engaged in a consultation and not to be disturbed. She glanced at me for a moment and away again and told him that it was extremely urgent.

"It's from the Central Police Station . . . a personal call for you, sir. It would be best to take it on my phone."

Dr Price was very put out by the interruption. He asked me to forgive him if he used the phone, but people were most inconsiderate. They rang him up morning, noon and night, and thought they had priority to break in on any consultation however important it was.

"Put the call through on my other phone, Margaret. I'll take it here."

Still she demurred and tried to get him out of the room and he scowled at her, till she went off and did as she was bid.

I watched his face as he spoke to the police.

"Dear me!" he said eventually and his hand went up to his bow tie. His face looked serious and sad and I remembered the day he had told me that both my parents were dead.

"Outright . . . " he said and then there was a long pause, while the voice at the police station chattered tinnily in his ear.

"Outright?" he said and looked graver than ever. "I'd better tell you that the lady in question is expecting a child. Urgent admission to a home might be the best thing. No, no, she has no near relatives. I'll see to it myself."

There was some more conversation and then he replaced the receiver and looked over at me absent-mindedly. I got to my feet and said I would slip away quietly, as it was obvious that something very urgent indeed had come up. He came to stand behind me and his hand pressed my shoulder to put me back in my seat . . .

"No, no, my dear. Sit where you are. I just want to talk to Margaret. I'll not be more than a moment."

Soon he was back again with a glass of water and capsules.

"Please to swallow both capsules, Lalage, with a draught of water," he said and I asked him in an interested voice what they were intended to do.

"Not any harm. Of that I assure you," he said and he took my hand and patted it, after the capsules were safely down.

"I want you to listen very carefully to what I am going to say to you now. In seven months, you will be delivered of an infant, a little boy perhaps, or a little girl, which will be a comfort to you in the years to come. It seems like the hand of God, that you should have a child at this particular time. You must never forget that the Almighty watches over you. No matter what you may be called upon to bear, it is by His will. Always . . . always, you are in his loving care . . . the child's life too. It's the most precious possession you have, this coming child. Unfortunately it is in its most critical stage. The slightest thing could deprive you of motherhood at this moment . . ."

I wondered if this was his pompous preamble to advice on ante-natal care, but I felt vaguely uneasy. Gareth was my most precious possession. The baby counted for nothing compared with Gareth.

"I want you to cling to the thought of your baby now, as a drowning man might cling to a straw. The child must uphold you . . . "

He took both my hands in his and held them tightly.

"I've always had a great affection for you, Lalage. Your father was my closest friend at Trinity. Your mother travelled all the way down from the house in Argyll, just so as I could have the honour of delivering you. It was the saddest day in my whole life, when I had to go over to the school that day and tell you they were both gone. You behaved with great bravery. I feel confident that you will do so again . . . "

He looked down at me and his face was desolate as he asked me if Gareth had been well, when he had left home. I was surprised at the question.

"He was fine."

Then I thought of the urgent call from

the Police Station, and 'outright' and the poor lady, who was expecting a baby, and some of the pieces of a dreadful jig-saw puzzle fell into position in my head, till I was numbed with the horror of it.

"That call was about Gareth," I whispered hoarsely and did not recognise the voice for my own. "He's had an accident. You said 'outright' and that means he's dead. Oh, God! Is Gareth dead?"

Even then he did not tell me, just shook his head sadly and asked me to remember what a sudden shock might do to Gareth's child, and I tried to work it out in a brain, that seemed unable to work anything out any more. Gareth had no child. I had wanted a baby, when we were first married and he had put it off from one year till the next . . . had said that babies were boring things and that they cluttered up one's life. I blurted it out to Dr Price now, and again he shook his head mournfully.

"Then let's both ensure that one day he will have a child. That is what he'd have wanted most in the world, and that you should be happy again, one day."

He was using a kind of past tense about Gareth. I had not really believed that he was dead, but I believed it at that moment and felt a chasm open before my feet. Then I told myself that it must be some dreadful nightmare and that presently I would wake up and put out my hand and feel him by my side . . . hear his gay, teasing voice telling me to wake up . . . hear him getting serious if I started to weep about it . . . saying "Did you dream it again, Lally, that old Price had come to tell you? Don't cry about it. You've still got me and I love you."

"Drink this, Mrs Kingston. It'll make you feel better."

The brandy was fire in my chest and Margaret's hand on my shoulder was encouragement and Dr Price was coming fussily across the room to sit on the desk and look down at me.

"I'd like to take you into the Wimpole right away . . . keep you there for a week or two. There's nobody of any use at the flat and you have no relatives to call upon in a crisis. To give the infant the best possible chance . . . nay, and I say this advisedly, any chance at all, I'd advise bed rest and sedation."

"But I must see Gareth . . . " I protested in a small whisper and he cut in across me with his brows knitted together and his mouth pursed in negation.

"That won't be necessary. Certainly not . . . under no condition would I allow it . . . most inadvisable."

"You said 'outright'. That's always 'killed outright'. It must have been an accident . . . "

I felt detached from what was happening in the room. Everything was as unreal as if I had wandered into some nightmare sequence. Perhaps it was the capsules, taking effect on me, but I felt as if I had floated up to the ceiling in some impossible way and could look down at myself, as I sat on the Chippendale chair, with Margaret taking the empty glass out of my hand.

"It was a street accident in the Haymarket," he told me shortly and still my stranger's voice went on with the questions.

"How did it happen?"

"He stepped off the pavement without

looking. The police think that his mind must have been elsewhere and that he forgot the one-way traffic."

"What hit . . . What . . . what . . . "

"You mustn't distress yourself about that point. He was killed instantly. He couldn't have had a moment of suffering."

"Are you sure . . . quite sure . . . ?"

"They said it was certain. You mustn't think about it."

It could not be Gareth who was dead. Gareth was always so alive and happy . . . full of quicksilver . . . sparkling like champagne. It could never be Gareth, who had joked about the verb 'to cherish', about how it meant that you must say 'I love you', every time you said 'goodbye' . . . and first thing in the morning and last thing at night . . . about how it meant that I had to prepare his toothbrush with my own, his the green and mine the pink. It did not matter if we got them mixed up. That was his acid test of love and now he was dead . . .

"The funeral . . . What about the funeral?"

"In the normal circumstances, Lalage,

you would now run the gauntlet of early widowhood, but if you do this at the moment, you'll condemn your child to death."

He had gone to sit behind the desk again and he watched me over the gold rims, his eyes sorry for my sorrow.

"In all seriousness, I say this to you. Make up your mind now if you want this child. It's a serious decision. Some people might feel that a widow would be less cumbered without pregnancy . . . "

I thought of Gareth and his hope of eternity and wondered if he had found out that Christianity was just a big confidence trick. I thought about his watch and his ring and his cigarette case and thought my throat would close before I got the words out.

"His personal effects . . . watch and ring. He was wearing them. Ask the police. I want them particularly . . . for his son . . . and I'll go into the home . . . "

He arranged it all in a nightmare sequence . . . took me there himself in his own car. The Matron met us at the door and did not meet my eyes. The lift man kept his face averted from mine. Then we were at a white painted door and there was a swinging tag on the brass handle saying DO NOT DISTURB. There was loneliness in the words and a great void. Then I was in the room and a nurse in a blue dress was walking across to meet me.

"God comfort you in your trouble, Mrs Kingston. We'll have to help you between us to find the silver lining to this cloud, that's come down on you."

She put me to bed and gave me an injection and Dr Price's voice boomed and faded. Then a long time after, I woke up and the curtains were drawn across the window and it must have been night, because there was no sound of traffic. I wondered where I was and then the whole truth overwhelmed me again. I searched the room for the nurse and found her.

"Perhaps I'll lose the baby. I'll just have selfishly left Gareth all by himself and slept here trying to forget him . . . and not able to forget him . . . "

"So you're awake at last?"

The nurse came over and stood at the

bed-side, smiling down at me.

"That was a powerful long sleep you had, right through a day and a night. You'll feel the better of it, especially when I've run a hot bath for you and put you into one of your own pretty nightdresses."

"I should have gone to see after things . . ." I whispered and she stood and shook her head at me, her hands on her hips.

"Now there's to be no such talk out of you. You've been a damn' sensible woman to make the decision you did. People might think it was the easy thing to do, but I realise what you gave up to come in here and never see him again . . ."

She sighed and put up a hand to the white cap, that perched like a starched butterfly on her brown hair.

"We won't talk about that end of it now," she decided and sat down on the edge of the bed, frowning a little, as if she was wondering what to say to me. After a bit, her hand came out to rest on my tummy.

"You've got a child in here . . . a

little child, that will grow up to be a man or a woman one day. By God's grace, it will fill the emptiness that's in your heart, but just now, it hasn't got a tight hold on life. It's crouching down in there, like the way a hare would be crouching in the long summer grass."

Her smile was bringing brightness into the gloom of the room. Then she was serious again.

"In a month or so, the child will have put down its roots. Then you'll not shift him, but just at this moment, we mustn't have anything that will jolt him out of his form . . . "

They all called her 'O'Brien' and over the next weeks, she and I got to know each other. When I looked for her, she was always at my side and she was never anything but cheerful. She had an oval face and dark brown hair, parted in the centre. Her voice was gentle and soft, with the mountain mists in it and the soft fresh breezes and the turf fires and the light cool lanes. Her hands were kind. She was very much what I imagined the Madonna must have been, but she was startled when I told her this late one night.

"If you draped a blue hood over your head, you might be Mary, the Mother of God."

She looked at me keenly out of her long-lashed blue eyes to see if I was in my right mind. Then she put back her head and laughed.

"God above! I've had compliments in my day, but that beats Banagher."

"Have you had a great many compliments, O'Brien?"

She saw I was dispirited and she was not going to have that.

"I've had a deal of things said about me, one way and another, Mrs Kingston, but I'll leave it to you to decide whether they were compliments or if they weren't."

She perched herself on the edge of the bed with a deep sigh, but the fun was sparkling in the back of her eyes.

"A fella once told me I walked in beauty like the night," she said, keeping her face very sober, except for the laugh in her eyes, and I remarked that he must have been a poetic sort of a man.

"He was not," she exclaimed indignantly. "I found out that all he wanted to do was to walk into my bed, so I asked him if he was thinking of walking up the aisle first of all, but it seemed that he wasn't."

"Oh, dear! Haven't you had any really nice things said to you?"

"Mothers say flattering things to you, when you put their baby into their arms for the first time. You have to be careful not to get too full of stinking pride, if you work in my sort of a job, for 'tis only the anaesthetic wearing off. Ah! I don't mind what people say to me, one way or the other. There was an old priest I knew one time at home. He said a thing to me that stuck in my head, for it was God's truth. He told me that a man is his own judge and jury. No matter what praise you get in this life . . . no matter what blame, you know inside in yourself, if it's right or not. It's yourself you've got to live with. There's no fooling yourself."

"There's no fooling yourself," I agreed.

She went to the mirror over the mantelpiece and looked at her reflection in silence for a full minute, turning her head this way and that and frowning a little.

"I'd make a rotten Virgin Mary," she decided at last in disgust and turned round to face me with her hands on her hips.

"I haven't enough patience with kids for a start . . . and my language is terrible too. It was my father, God rest his soul He was always swearing at Mother and at us kids and I got into the habit of it early on. Ah, no, Mrs Kingston, apart from general unworthiness, I'd be a rotten Virgin. Ten to one, I'd let out and give the Infant Jesus a slap on the backside and then the fat would be in the fire up in heaven."

I thought of the skill and the patience with which she practised her art and of the warm kindness she had shown me and I knew that there were plenty of women in the world, who might be far less worthy of the part I had suggested for her. She was Irish to the backbone. Her roots were still firmly planted in the Bog of Allan, like one of the rowan trees, that flourish in Ireland. She called them 'quicken trees' and she told me all about her native land in the days that followed. As I listened to her voice, I could smell the turf fires and the peppery smell of the gorse. I could see the brightness of the island sky and hear the soft accents of the people. It would be so like my beloved Argyll. She coaxed me to speak to her about the Highlands and the time slid away from beneath us, day after day, and I found it possible to live again and not turn my face to the wall and pray for death.

Dr Price was pleased with my progress too. One day, he told me I was well enough to see my solicitor, and old Mr Hood came creeping in like a tortoise, to pat my hand and tell me that the whole thing was over and that I was not to worry about financial matters. When the estate was wound up, I would be a tolerably wealthy woman, for by a stroke of good fortune, Gareth had taken out ample insurance on hearing that a child was expected. Mr Hood's voice was as dry as dust as it went on and on. I would know, of course, that Gareth had had money of his own and I could keep up my present standards of life . . . or virtually so. In addition, by a strange coincidence, I had fallen heir to an Irish country estate in County Cork. A cousin of Gareth's had been killed in an accident a few days previous to Gareth's death. The house, which was called Cool-na-Grena would now revert to me.

Cool-na-Grain-ya, I thought to myself, and remembered Dr Price's waiting-room and the notice in the *Telegraph*, while Mr Hood's voice buzzed on and on like the fly, that had buzzed against the window pane that day . . .

There would be death duties, of course, but the Irish estate was worth very little. The house was very old. It was the family residence of that branch of the O'Connell Kingstons and it was in poor repair. It was mortgaged for three thousand pounds with the National Bank of Ireland.

It was very warm in the room and O'Brien had turned on the fan. It made a whirring noise and turned its face first one way and then the other and sent small currents of air towards the bed every half minute. The whole thing, Mr Hood was telling me, house, land and furniture would about cover the mortgage and leave me with a few hundred pounds in hand. The O'Connell Kingstons were all gone now except for my unborn child and this was but a poor heritage for him. The sensible thing to do would be to auction the whole place as it stood and not to worry my head about it. He had got the local solicitor in Ballyboy to send him a report on the property and he would give me a detailed description on it. He handed me a typed letter and said I should read it at my leisure. He was a fatherly old man. He stood up and went to look out of my window and then he came back to sit by the bed — hemmed and hawed for a while and then said what he must do next might cause me pain and he was sorry for it. He gave me a manilla envelope, sealed with red wax and I saw that it must contain the things I had asked Dr Price to get from the police.

"I'll leave you alone, my dear Lalage," he said, stroking my cheek for an instant with a dry, parchment, old hand. Then he went quietly from the room and I picked up the solicitor's report and knew myself for a coward, for I was only postponing the pain of opening the manilla envelope and seeing Gareth's things again.

The letter was a very friendly one and it told me all I wanted to know about the family house of the O'Connell Kingstons. It was solidly built and was situated in a favourable position about two hundred yards from the sea, in its own grounds on the coast of County Cork. It was in poor repair and the land too had been neglected. It would take a great deal of money to repair and modernise the house. There was more detailed information, but I skimmed through it quickly, thinking all the time of Gareth's watch and his ring and his gold cigarette case in the envelope at my hand. I had no interest in the house. It could go to the highest bidder. There was a local builder who was keen to buy it lock, stock and barrel, for the land was well wooded and he wanted the timber. He planned to fell the trees and demolish the house, sell off its bricks and slates for whatever they would fetch and turn the place into a timber yard . . .

I picked up the envelope, opened it, took out the contents, wrapped in tissue paper . . . the gold watch, the cigarette case. I snapped the case open and read my own writing engraved inside.

WITH ALL MY LOVE, LALAGE.

Last of all, I unwrapped the signet ring and slipped it on my finger, looked at the crest, the phoenix, rising from its own ashes and underneath the scroll with the single word RESURGAM.

"I will arise again," I whispered. "I will arise again."

For the first time since his death, I began to weep. I lay across the bed, clutching at the coverlet with my nails and I wept bitter, bitter tears. I was alone, or so I thought. There was nobody to hear me, but after a time, I heard O'Brien's voice, calm and even.

"Mr Hood told me he had come about the baby's inheritance. Wouldn't you like to tell me about it?"

I waved my hand at the cigarette case, that lay on the bed at my side and she picked it up and opened it.

"L-A-L-A-G-E," she spelt out. "How would you say that?"

"Lal-a-jee," I muttered.

"Isn't that a lovely name to have? It's like a bit of poetry put to music, isn't it . . . and it suits you fine."

She picked up the watch and held it against her ear.

"The watch keeps good time and the ring fits your finger fine. You'll have to mind these things carefully, but it wasn't them I was interested in. I wanted to hear about Cool-na-Grena. Mr Hood thought it was a queer name for a house to have, but any Irish person would know it. You often get houses with the same name in Ireland. It means a corner in the sun . . . and Mr Hood told me that this place was by the sea as well. Come on now, Mrs Kingston! I'll sponge your face and hands and we'll put some Cologne on your forehead. Then you can sit over by the window, where it's cooler and tell me the whole thing."

"It's on the coast of County Cork," I told her, as she dabbed the Cologne out on my handkerchief and her face lit up with enthusiasm.

"God above! That's a bit of luck. That'll be a heritage to be proud of . . . for your son and your son's son too . . . a fine house looking out over the Atlantic."

I asked her if she was familiar with that part of the country, but I only did it out of politeness, for I had no interest in it. I sat by the window and watched the square of blue sky, trapped between the high roofs of the town houses.

"I know it well. The sea is beautiful there. You can stand on the shore and watch the big ships come creeping out of Cove on their way to America."

"This house is dilapidated, O'Brien. It's mortgaged for three thousand pounds and it's falling to pieces. It's no good to anybody, except for the trees that grow on the land. There's a timber merchant willing to buy it and he'll fell the trees and turn it into a timber yard."

She stood at the window looking down into the street.

"If it's mortgaged, that means there's money borrowed on it, doesn't it? You'd have to put down three thousand pounds, before it was yours. It's an awful lot of money to find."

"The mortgage wouldn't worry me," I told her. "But I can't be bothered with a house, that's nothing but a pile of ruins, away in some God-forsaken place."

She asked me if I had ever been to Ireland and I said that I had not.

"The coast of Cork is a lovely place . . . " she mused, and she was not in the room any more, but away in her native land again.

"It's all gentle and green . . . and all little hills and brown country roads, that go round and round and never get anywhere. Into a man's haggard a road would take you, all among the hens and the ducks, and when you think you've made a mistake, doesn't it take a twist round the end of the house and off you go again to wind in between the green hills. There's lovely sandy shores . . . and farms tucked in the valleys . . . and the people have soft voices, that go up and down and about like their own roads. They're kind and their hearts are warm. They would take a woman in trouble like yourself to those same warm hearts. They'd stretch out their arms to welcome home the heir to Cool-na-Grena himself."

She stood opposite me and shook her head at me in reproof.

"I wouldn't be turning my back on a corner in the sun, Mrs Kingston. I'd go over there and I'd claim my child's heritage, if I had to sell the shirt off my back to do it . . . and that's no lie."

I told Mr Hood that I could not make up my mind about Cool-na-Grena. I argued with myself about it, first one way and then the other, during the long empty days that followed. Then finally I decided that there would be no harm if I just went over and looked at it, but I knew in my heart that I was doing it to fill in time. It was O'Brien, who 'sold' Ireland to me in the finish, though I drove a hard bargain with her, for I demanded a personally conducted tour.

"If you'll come with me, I'll fly to Shannon and we'll hire a car and drive out to the estate. If you're so set on my seeing the place, then I'll see it, but I'm telling you before I go, that it's almost certain I'll turn straight round and come home again."

"Very well, honey, if that's the only way you'll do it, but don't talk about coming home again. You'll be going home, when you're going to Cool-na-Grena."

So one fine day, a few weeks later, with O'Brien at my side, I landed at Shannon and went straight to the hotel in Limerick, where Dr Price insisted I should rest.

2

Cool-Na-Grena

THE next day it was sunny and bright, with the smoke in straight plumes from each cottage chimney, as we drove the long winding way to Cool-na-Grena. They were expecting us there . . . a man called Gregory, who was a resident steward and two women. The steward had been taken on by Cousin Dermot, just before the accident and I knew nothing about him, nor about the others. I was to decide their fate, when I decided my own and I was pretty abject about the future, when the car pulled up at a black gate, after what I thought might be an endless journey, that went on and on, and never came to anywhere.

I climbed out from behind the wheel of the car and joined O'Brien in front of the rather magnificent gated entrance. Somebody had evidently been working on the pillars, for there was fresh concrete between the grey stones. The gates were newly painted too and the name had been picked out in gold leaf in a very pleasing way.

We strolled along the drive, till it wound away round a grassy hill. I stood there with the smell of the gorse peppery in my nostrils and felt that the place was welcoming me. Behind us, three miles back, was a range of mountains, all purples and gold and dark browns, with the shadows of the clouds chasing across them.

"We'd better get on, I suppose," I said, and made my way towards the car, but O'Brien demurred at that.

"We're early yet. We said four and it's not three. They'll hardly be ready for an hour or so."

"An hour won't make any difference. They've had weeks to prepare for us."

I pressed the starter and turned the car into a drive, scarcely wide enough for it. Once we were round the little hill, there were trees on both sides, as we came through a fair-sized wood. We were in a tunnel of green leaves, that seemed to twist and turn till we had lost all sense of direction, when it shot us out into glaring sunshine, with the sea far below us on the left and the house on the right. I drove round the sweep and pulled up at the bottom of a flight of steps, that led up to the front door. Then I got out and stuck my hands deep in my pockets, as I looked up for the first time at the façade of Cool-na-Grena.

It was far larger than I had expected . . . an imposing looking residence. The steps were uneven and somebody had been working to gouge out the weeds and moss from between the flags. The green stuff had been left in a pile on the drive. The windows were clean, the paintwork fresh. The front door had character. It had a brass dolphin for a knocker, which was a small sun in its own right. I turned my back on it and looked down at the immense expanse of ocean . . . had to narrow my eyes to its glitter.

"A corner in the sun, O'Brien. I like it."

"Thanks be to God!" breathed O'Brien. "I've been out of my mind the whole way here that you'd turn round and clear off . . . say I'd brought you on a fool's errand."

There was no reply when we knocked, so we walked round the side of the house to the back door, but we got no answer there either and O'Brien gave it her considered opinion that all the occupants of the house were dead drunk or had been murdered in their beds. The yard might have been a junk yard from the number of rusted tins and old bicycles and derelict bed frames, that lay scattered about it. I wondered grimly what the steward had been up to, to let it get in such a state, but O'Brien championed him.

"He'd have other things to see to in a place the size of this. He hasn't been here long enough yet for you to judge. Don't worry your head about the old yard. I'll soon get it tidied up for you."

Round at the front of the house again, I was wishing I had put on a summer dress. There was no doubt that the name suited it. O'Brien had advised slacks and a finger-tip reefer jacket, which was her idea of suitable maternity wear. It concealed the fact that my waist was not quite so slim as formerly, but it was far too warm. There was the sound of water, deliciously cool, somewhere to the left and we decided to explore. In half a minute we found what the staff were doing . . . building a waterfall.

The original stream must have wandered down the hillside aimlessly, but some would-be engineer had devised a dam higher up. It was a clever idea and it must have taken huge effort to get the boulders positioned. There was one last giant stone to be slotted into place and then the water must fall ten feet down into a natural basin. We came on the project over the brow of a hill. The steward and his two helpers were totally absorbed. The older woman was standing on the bank of the stream, holding like grim death to a rope, which was fastened to the stone and the stone was still poised in the air. The younger woman was in the bed of the stream in bare legs, her dress tucked inside navy knickers, with a French Foreign Legion effect . . . Her hair had come down round her face and shoulders and she was spattered with mud from head to foot.

The man was very dark . . . in his thirties as far as I could judge. He was straddled across the water with a foot on each of two ledges, in a perilous position, easing the boulder to its key point. They did not hear us draw closer with the sound of the water. I raised an eyebrow at O'Brien and remarked that it was obvious why nobody had answered the door to us and she put her arm through mine and grinned at me.

"Don't look at it like that," she coaxed. "Think of the trouble they're taking to make it look pretty for you. Isn't that a better way to see it? God help them! They don't look very prosperous."

I walked across to the top of what would soon be the fall, if all went well and my hands were stuffed deep in my jacket pockets as I studied the grave intense face of the man. He was totally absorbed in his dangerous task. Then he lifted his eyes and saw me . . . said something to the others and they dropped everything in panic. The boulder splashed into place far too quickly. There was a howl from the young woman as she sat down heavily in the muddy bed of the stream. The new cascade of the fall hit the man on the chest with full force and he was gone into the pool below. I peered down and saw him clambering out on the edge of it, soaked to the skin and I was very relieved that he had not been killed in such a tumble . . . not even hurt, by the look of him.

The older woman kept her head. She walked over to me and curtsied, told me she was Hannah.

"Welcome home!" she smiled. "Welcome home, Ma'am. Mr Gareth's lady is welcome to Cool-na-Grena. It's ashamed of myself I am, that you find us in the state we're in this minute, but look at the grand waterfall, we're after making for you."

I put out my hand to take hers and she wiped her hand down her dress before she gave it to me.

"Don't be fretting about Mr Gregory now," she told me. "Sure, he can swim like a trout."

The young girl gave a nervous laugh and put her muddy hand to her mouth, as she was introduced as Mary Bridget Hanratty.

The dark man appeared up the slope, wringing the water out of the bottom of his jersey, shaking his head like a water-spaniel, as I looked at him apologetically.

"I'm afraid I came upon you suddenly. I'm sorry, Gregory . . . Mr Gregory. There's some confusion about your name. Mr Hood said your surname was Gregory . . ."

"You'd better call me Gregory. Everybody else does."

Mary Bridget Hanratty giggled at that for some secret reason of her own and he frowned at her briefly, while I tried to thank them for the waterfall.

"You've gone to so much trouble and it's wonderful, but I don't know whether I'm going to stay here."

O'Brien took my arm at that and I saw that I had said the wrong thing . . . the un-Irish thing, as she put it.

"I'm the nurse," she informed them bluntly. "My name is O'Brien and I'm sorry we came on ye so early, but herself is taken with punctuality. I couldn't hold her back, she was that anxious to get here. Anyway we'll go below to the strand now and do a spot of exploring . . . let you get straightened out up here. We'll arrive officially in an hour or two . . . "

Only Mary Bridget Hanratty looked embarrassed now as she climbed out on the bank of the stream and O'Brien was equal to the situation, for she pulled the dress out of the knickers and down about her and patted her shoulder.

"You remind me of a young one I saw at the flicks . . . working in the paddy fields, in Italy or somewhere. God knows! There was a volcano anyway and she was full of sex appeal. Every time she fell in the mud, all the boy-os in the picture house used to whistle and cheer. I don't know if the same would apply to you, but I think it might be as well if you went into the house and had a rub-down, before you catch your death of cold."

"You should both have a soak in a hot bath," I advised. "We'll stay down on the beach for an hour or so. There's no hurry."

They all looked mildly surprised and I saw that the code of hot baths might not apply to this forsaken spot. O'Brien was tugging at my sleeve to urge me to go down along the path to the sea with her and I sensed that she was afraid what I might say next. We walked along the springy soft turf to the pointed headland, where the ground fell steeply away, to a sandy shore on the left and to rocks on the right. There were steps on both sides made of old railway sleepers and we went on down to the sandy shore and found a perfect little bay. The sand was soft and golden and deep, but as we approached the sea, it grew hard and firm and the waves were creaming at our feet, curling and foaming in their eternal beauty.

"So this is the Atlantic?" I muttered, with no happiness in my words, but only bitterness and loneliness, so that O'Brien adopted her bracing manner with me forthwith. She told me that we must earn our keep and by that she meant that we must collect driftwood and pile it at the bottom of the steps and it was as good an occupation as any to fill up the emptiness of time. I wandered away from her and picked up a piece of wood here and a piece there, while I listened to the lonely voice of the sea. At the end of an hour, I was suddenly completely exhausted, physically and mentally and wanted to do nothing, but lie down upon my bed and turn my face to the wall.

"Let's go back to the house," I suggested and she looked at me scornfully.

"Are you mad?" she demanded. "This is the land of the free, where time was made for slaves. We'll have to give them a minute or two yet. They won't have had time to scrape the mud off Mary Bridget Hanratty, let alone do what has to be done in the house."

"Please," I muttered and she looked at my face and in a moment, her arm was round my waist and she was scolding me that I had not told her I was dead on my feet. She put my coat over her arm and we went up the steps and across two hundred yards of hungry sea grass to the front door. They must have been watching for us from the windows, for Gregory came out to the top step to greet us, wearing faded canvas slacks and a white roll-top sweater. His hair was dry now, but as black as ever and falling in an unruly lock over his forehead. There was an unmistakable nautical look about him. His teeth were very white against the old mahogany of his skin as he smiled at us.

"We seem to have got things organised at last, Mrs Kingston."

He put his hand on the knob of the door to the left and smiled at me again.

"Would you like to come into the sitting-room and have tea, or would you prefer Hannah to show you up to your room?"

I walked into the sitting-room and it was bare and without comfort. I could think of no word to say to him as I went to the window to look down on the magnificent panorama of sea and sky, and behind my back I heard O'Brien filling in for me again.

"We've been collecting driftwood below on the strand, Gregory. God knows how we'll get it up here, but if we did, it would keep us in fires for a week."

"Mary Bridget and I will soon fetch it up," he told her and I turned away from the window and walked across to the fireplace, where they had lit a fire to air the room . . . a fire of peat, like it had been in the old days in Argyll, with the same nostalgic smell to it and the old warmth in its glow. I was in a strung-up state, as I always seemed to be and my eyes filled with tears. I was furious with myself and I kept my back to the room and forgot all about the mirror over the mantelpiece, till I met Gregory's eyes in it, as I brushed at my face impatiently.

"Mary Bridget?" I said and forced myself to think what might happen in civilised England, if one asked the housemaid to carry up wood from the sea.

"Oh, I know she's supposed to do the housework," he smiled and raised one eyebrow as if he invited me to see the funny side of it. "But she's worth two men if you let her work outside."

I turned round to face him.

"And inside?" I asked stiffly, and again came the quick smile and the lifted brow.

"As long as you don't frighten her, she'll be fine. She's bringing in the tea now."

As he spoke, she came into the room, bottom first, as she pushed the door open. Then she turned about to present a scarlet face and bedraggled wispy hair. She had an enormous silver tray in her hands, which was set out with an assortment of crockery, including a large brown tea-pot.

"Tea is served," she said with a giggle and Gregory frowned at her as he took the tray from her hands and put it on a low table, pulled up a chair for me and waited for me to pour out. A dreadful tension was building up in the room and then Gregory's eye fell on the plate of sandwiches, which would have provided ample nourishment for men working in the fields. They consisted of thick cuts of ham between half inch slices of bread.

"I told her to take off the crusts," he muttered to Mary's disappearing back.

"For God's sake, Gregory!" cried O'Brien. "This isn't the Ritz and Mrs Kingston doesn't think it is. A day might come, when we'd all be glad of a few crusts . . . "

She picked up a plate that was far too small for the big cake it carried and asked us if it wasn't a sight for sore eyes.

"And how did ye guess it was Mrs Kingston's favourite?" she demanded and just stopped short of giving me a nudge, for it seemed she was as anxious for them to like me as she had been for me to like the house.

"I love 'seedy cake'," I murmured and took in the desolation of the whole room with a sigh. They had made the best of it. They had stained and polished the bare boards. They had cut a piece of old carpet to make a solitary mat. The furniture was old and shabby with springs poking out from under the chairs. There was a mahogany table in one of the windows and a vase of chrysanthemums, very clumsily arranged, with copper beech leaves and no art whatsoever. The paper was faded and old, but O'Brien was taking stock too.

"If you were to get a few rolls of paper in Cork, I'd do this room up till you'd not know it. I'm a great hand at interior decorating . . . and your sitting room carpet beyond in London would fit this room a treat . . . and your suite of furniture . . . those chairs with the ears . . . "

"It's being stored," I said flatly. "It's to be sold."

"That's a crying shame," she said without any finer feelings whatever. "It would have made a grand room."

Then she laughed and told me to eat up my seedy cake and indeed I finished every crumb of the big slice Gregory cut for me. I was not a little surprised at myself for I had had no appetite since Gareth's death. Gregory passed the cups and drank his own tea and ate nothing at all and I knew he was highly nervous of me. Yet he was a polished sort of man to be a farm steward. His manners were impeccable and there was a sophistication about him. Then presently tea was over and Hannah was suggesting a tour of the house. Mary Bridget Hanratty appeared from somewhere and fell in behind us as we walked across the hall to the dining room. It matched the sitting room in size and the furnishings were best junk-shop here too. The dining table was square with bulbous legs and it was adorned by a jamjar of marigolds, which could only have been arranged by the same hand as the flowers in the sitting room. The curtains were heavy chenille velvet and I caught one of them to draw it across the window. Gregory stretched out his hand too late to stop me and the next second it crashed down, missing my head by a postage stamp width, with its heavy pole. I stood there with half the curtain in my hand.

"You want to be careful," O'Brien warned me dryly. "You might have dashed your brains out. Still it's a reminder of the red damask curtains over in London. They'd fit these windows a treat . . . fittings and all. We could jettison the old poles. The red carpet would fit this room too. I just stepped it out with my eye."

Gregory was put out about the curtain pole. There was a misery that lived in the whiteness of his face, even under his tan. I felt sorry for them all suddenly. They might have people dependent on them and their jobs depended on me. They might go hungry if I turned my back on Cool-na-Grena. Yet, I was strangely averse to leave. It was country too like my native Argyll. It had warmth of soul about it and friendliness.

"I could paper this room," O'Brien was dreaming, but I knew by the flat voice that she had lost her hopes. She was more sure of it than ever when I picked up the carpet and it tore in my hand . . .

The morning room was full of worm-eaten furniture and had two panes broken in the window and repaired by ply. The kitchen at the back was gloomy and immense, with a black monster of a stove and a Victorian copper, a deal dresser, a white scrubbed table. The room was spotless. I will say that for it, but what a labour it must have been. There were copper pots and saucepans, that gleamed.

"I've got all sorts of kitchen stuff," I said almost to myself " . . . A washing machine and spin dryer . . . fridge . . . electric cooker . . . mixer . . . This floor is awful, but we had the same problem in Scotland in the old days. We covered it with concrete and laid tiles. You'd never believe the change it made. It only wanted a wipe over . . . I have a polisher too. We could polish the tiles. It's like magic . . . switch on and walk beside it . . . "

The hall flags were scrubbed white

and it was probably the best part of the house. I teased O'Brien, as she opened her mouth.

"Yes, I know. If I were to buy a few rolls of paper in Cork. Does your union let you do that sort of work?"

At my side, Mary Bridget Hanratty's red face appeared.

"I could do the kitchen floor," she whispered. "Least of all, I could with my father to help me. He's used to tiling and that. We did the floors at home, but tiles and cement is dear . . . "

She got redder than ever as I thanked her. I called her Mary but she said she was never called anything but Mary Bridget . . . and so we made our way up an unspeakable carpet to the top landing, where there was nothing but bare boards . . . and the echoes of our feet.

The six bedrooms were grim. I had the room over the sitting room and it could have been superb. As it was, it was wretched. A brass bedstead, that was not old enough to be attractive was smothered in a feather bed and yellowing blankets, covered with a white counterpane, that might have concealed a corpse for all its comfort. There was a wash-hand stand with a china basin and a chipped enamel jug.

"The jug of that got broken a while back," Hannah said and Mary Bridget proclaimed her guilt by putting her hand to her mouth.

There were more marigolds on the dressing table and I could not resist the temptation to give them a twitch here and a pull there till they looked happy. In the glass, I saw them looking at me approvingly. Then I went through to a dressing-room off the main bedroom and planned to myself to make it a bathroom . . . and remembered that I had not decided to stay . . .

Along the landing there was a family bathroom with an enormous bath-shaped bath. It would take gallons of water even to half fill it. The basin was a period piece. The lavatory was elevated to a dais for some reason of plumbing, not for grandeur. It had an overhead tank, complete with a piece of string and a china handle. I pulled the handle, much to Mary Bridget's shame and the tank growled at me like a dog, but produced no water. Gregory murmured at my side that "it went back on you now and again and you had to give it a sharp tug." I did this and of course, it came away in my hand. He took the handle and was very grim about it, said he would see to it later on . . .

I planned to make two bathrooms out of this huge one . . . asked him about the capacity of the stove and again I was struck by the anxiety in his eyes, that I might not leave my inheritance.

"The bath problem is difficult," he admitted. "It's a Heath-Robinson affair downstairs and we must have a new stove in the future. It's hopeless as it is . . . "

The bedrooms were gaunt and ugly and the furniture was only fit for the fire. The walls were damp and I was apprehensive of the state the roof might be in and I asked Gregory about it.

"There were some tiles off after the big storm, but I fixed them. It's quite sound up there now."

We went down into the hall again and I asked him if the outbuildings were in as bad a condition as the house.

"Outbuildings?" he asked blankly, but Hannah was ready with the answer.

"There's the barn," she put in. "But the roof's gone in on it . . . and the hen house is all to pieces too. The hens would sooner roost in the bushes anyhow and I don't know if they're any the worse off for it, for they never laid well at the best of times."

"Do you keep any pigs?"

"We got rid of the old sow after Mr Dermot was killed," Mary Bridget said sadly. "Maybe we could buy a few bonhams cheap? I love pigs."

I had liked Mary Bridget at once and I could see that Gregory was right about her. If I stayed on, I would make a 'man' out of her, for she was wasted cutting ham sandwiches. I was a country girl myself, born and bred, and I felt an itch to get those hens organised . . . an itch to buy some more pigs and start afresh.

"My father can put in plumbing," Mary Bridget volunteered, a hand at her mouth again. "He put in the central heating for the Colonel above . . . and the new bathroom there and all. Sure, they have three baths at the big house.

Father could fix your new stove and the baths, as easy as wink. I'd have to give him a hand with the heavy work, but I'd be glad to . . . carrying the bath and that."

"That sounds wonderful, Mary Bridget. You solve all my difficulties for me."

It was the polite social thing to say and I said it automatically. Then I realised just how wonderful it really was. The pain I had had for the last eight weeks, in every waking moment, was gone.

"I'll think it over tonight. It's best to sleep on important decisions. I'll tell you what I make up my mind to do tomorrow morning. Just for now, I'll have a bath and change for supper."

Gregory looked doubtfully at me as I went up the stairs and warned me that the bath water was 'not too good'. Indeed, I found that this was an understatement. I undressed and went along to the bathroom in my red housecoat, but when I turned on the hot tap, there was a choking coughing gasp and a trickle of water and rust and soot. After a bit, it increased its rate of flow, but by the time the water was clear, it was as cold as if I had drawn it from a spring well. I filled the bath and jumped in and out again, thinking what a task I was setting myself, if I undertook to make anything of the property, yet it was a challenge . . .

I dressed in navy blue slacks and a silk shirt, that was slit up the side, and had a high collar. I felt like a Chinese lady as I went back down the stairs, in no way decided what to do. The whole estate was neglected, yet Gregory was not to blame. He was responsible for the gold leaf on the gates, for the steps to the beach . . . for the outside paintwork . . . probably the flowers. Without being told, I knew this was so. They had done their best against impossible odds.

I was at fault. I was obsessed with my own private disaster and was drowning in self-pity. The time had come for me to cry 'Halt' and to see if work was an antidote to tears. It seemed an impossibility now to rebuild the fortunes of the house, but I would have a shot at it. All at once I made my decision.

It would be a monument to Gareth and the house would arise again. It would arise from its own ashes, like the phoenix on Gareth's signet ring on my finger.

3

We Make A Beginning

THE baby moved for the first time with the faintest flickering as I made my decision. I sat down by the fire in the sitting room and knew that there were two of us now, Gareth's child and I. Then Mary Bridget edged in round the door in her apologetic way, wringing her hands like two pink dishcloths, her hair wisping about her hot face.

"I only wanted to do the fire," she said and put an unnecessary piece of peat on it, giving it an ungraceful kick with her foot as she turned round to look at me.

"It's the kitchen floor. You're worrying about tiles and that, but my father's get them cheap from Molloy, the contractor. Come to that, we could get broken tiles and piece them together. It would only be the cement then . . . "

I got to my feet and brushed back the

straggling hair from her forehead.

"Are you afraid I'll go away from Cool-na-Grena? Are you afraid it will go to the rats and the jackdaws?"

"You won't go away, Ma'am. I knew it the minute I seen you beyond at the fall. Sure, where would you go to and this your home?"

She got herself out of the room at last, bobbing and weaving like a shadow boxer and Hannah came in, looking very severe in a black dress. She tut-tutted about the fire and the fact that Mary Bridget had not swept the hearth.

"If you were worried about the repairs, Ma'am, I have a bit saved up in the Post Office. It's not a large sum . . . about fifty pounds. You could have it and welcome . . . and there's no need for you to pay me wages. Mr Dermot often couldn't manage it . . . "

I could not speak if I had to speak to live.

"I've been with the family since I was twelve years old," she went on in a soft voice. "You're the last of the O'Connell Kingstons and a high proud family they was . . . all dead and gone now. I'd not have you turned from Cool-na-Grena, not for my heart's blood."

"I'm not the last of the O'Connell Kingstons, Hannah. God has been good to me . . ."

I pulled the silk shirt tight against my stomach and smiled at her.

"Didn't they tell you I'm expecting a child . . . and every night I pray that it's a son."

If I had told her that she had inherited a million pounds, there could not have been any greater change in her.

"It's not true," she whispered, with the tears starting in her eyes. "It's not true."

"I'm to go over to London to have him and I'll bring him home to Cool-na-Grena for ever."

"God be praised!" she said with the tears splashing down her old wrinkled face. "God be praised!"

She spun round then and ran out of the room with her hands to her face and I wondered if Gregory would be the next to come in, for there was a pattern about the whole thing . . . and indeed in he came in five minutes or so and I saw that Hannah must have told him the news because his face was happy. His eyes went down to my middle for a second and then up again to my face and he stood just inside the door and looked across the room at me, where I stood by the fire like a Chinese mandarin.

"So you've heard the news?" I said at last, for he did not say anything, only stood there, looking at me.

"Don't worry if it's not a boy," he said and mighty awkwardly too, speaking very slowly as if he felt his way along from one phrase to the next.

"A little girl would be just as good. Don't set your heart on a son. I'm glad you're not going away . . . "

He went across to the window and I essayed a joke to ease the tension that was building up in the room.

"If you're thinking of drawing the curtains, Gregory, remember what happened in the room across the way."

He might not have heard me for all the notice he took of that. He kept his back turned to me and looked down at the sea and his voice was very gentle and soft.

"I thought the moment I set eyes

on you, that you were the person the old house has been waiting for, for thirty years. I knew I was right, when you arranged those flowers in the bowl upstairs. If you have any worries, I'd be glad to share them. Put your troubles on my shoulders. They're broad ones. I have a bit of money . . . not a tremendous fortune, but enough. Life can be hell for a woman left on her own . . . and you've never had to fend for yourself . . . always had somebody to look out for you . . . your father . . . your husband . . . If you want my help, you've only to ask . . ."

I knew by the set of his shoulders that he was embarrassed by having said so much to me. There was silence in the room, except for the hissing of the wood on the fire and the ticking of the clock on the mantelpiece. This was a strange farm steward indeed, I thought to myself. There was more to him than met the eye, and he was gentle and kind. I wondered what he was doing in such a job as he held at Cool-na-Grena. I knew the salary he received from Mr Hood once a month and by the look of him, he could have earned four times the amount in any executive position. He turned round slowly, smiling with relief that the difficult part of the interview was at an end.

"And don't worry if it's a little girl."

"Why do you work here?" I challenged him. "You're not an ordinary farm steward."

And now he would not meet my eye any more but looked down at the polished chestnut toes of his brogues.

"Indeed I am, and very ordinary too."

I thanked him very much for his offer of help and told him I would be very glad of his support and advice and presently he took himself off again and after a while, O'Brien came in and I wondered if she was going to conform to the general pattern . . . and indeed she did. It was obvious that the news that I had decided to stay on in Ireland had not reached her ears. She walked into the room and stood in the centre under the electric light bulb, her hands thrust down into the pockets of her dress in a most ungraceful way, that pushed her apron out in front of her like a starched flag. She was feeling awkward too and that was an unusual state for O'Brien, who was always in control of every situation. I imagined that I knew what she was going to say to me and as it turned out, I was not far wrong.

"I don't know how well off you are," she fired off at me like a shot out of a pistol, without any preamble. "But you're a widow and your husband was only young. He can't have had time to amass a fortune . . . and places like the Wimpole cost a fortune nowadays, to say nothing of the doctors' fees on top of that again. Tell me it's no business of mine, if you like. Tell me to go to hell and I won't hold it against you. I have a proposition to put to you. You can say 'yes', or you can say 'no'. It will make no difference between us two. We'll forget I made it. Now, I've been wanting a holiday for the last few years and not been able to afford one. I'd be in Ireland too and I'm never at ease anywhere else . . . though I'd not admit that to anybody else but yourself. Put me up here till the baby's born. I'd paper a few rooms to pass the time. I can do all sorts of things, you'd never dream of . . . "

I murmured that I was sure she could, but she only told me she could milk a cow, though I wouldn't think it to look at her.

"To look at you, O'Brien, I'd think you capable of almost anything."

"It's no joke," she said severely. "I'd be on holiday and doing no proper nursing work, so there would be no salary. If you could manage my keep . . . "

I leaned my forehead on the mantelpiece and after a while I had recovered sufficiently to tell her that I'd make a bargain with her.

"Stay on here till you want to go. You'll have to accept your salary, but don't worry about that, for it's covered by insurance . . . "

I got that ball past her and turned her onto the choosing of the wallpaper and what fun it would be . . . and then was surprised that I hoped to have fun ever again. Then she was talking about my furniture and begging me to have it sent over.

"It's only wood and cloth and horsehair. It's not alive. You know what a difference it would make to everyone in this house.

Think of the washing machine and the Hoover for a start. Put yourself in Mary B.'s shoes and think of getting down to that bloody copper in the corner . . ."

I was being selfish. There was no doubt about it. I gave in suddenly and promised to send for it. Then she told me she had anticipated my surrender and had taken the measurements of every room in the house. Then Gregory was in with sherry on a tray and odd glasses, one of which was genuine old Waterford. I bethought the decanter in the dining room, standing in its silver potato ring and I took myself off and fetched it, decanted the sherry and replaced the decanter in the gentleness of old silver, thinking how I must clutch at every beautiful thing I could find, if I was to resurrect this house to its old glory. Gregory was asking my advice about supper.

"Hannah has fried some chops and there's potatoes in their jackets . . . rice pudding to follow. I hope you find it all right. It's very plain. We're no hand at anything remotely elaborate."

I decided to serve the potatoes in the

silver rings, wrapped in a white napkin and hoped it would add some grace to the table. They had spread the cloth in the dining room, but the linen was threadbare and inadequate in size and the big forks had crooked prongs. The silver had almost certainly been given away free at the grocer's. Gregory pulled out my chair for me and took his place at my right hand and Mary Bridget came in at the double with two white dinner plates. On each of them was a pair of lamb chops, a pile of boiled cabbage and gravy, that lapped round Mary Bridget's thumb.

She put one plate down in front of me and the other in front of O'Brien, gave a sigh of relief and wiped her thumbs down the sides of her apron.

"Will ye take milk with the dinner . . . or will ye be drinking whiskey?"

I told her we would like water and she dashed out of the room like a retriever. She was back in a minute with Gregory's plate, three tumblers of water and the silver potato ring.

"Who but yourself would have thought of serving potatoes up in the decanter stand?" she said with great approval. "I never seen such elegant potatoes in my whole life."

There was nothing wrong with the cooking. Hannah put her head round the door a while later and I was able to tell her "the chops were all right". She confessed that she had been terrified that they were 'bloody' and she served the rice pudding herself, poured creamy country milk over it . . . and I was back in Argyll again . . .

There was so much to do . . . the papering, the hot water system . . . the outside ground . . . Could I put it all out to a contractor? I might manage to be able to pay the bills. It would be a worry. Besides, the other way was the way of choice. It seemed that helpers had sprung from the ground like dragons' teeth. I had Mary Bridget's father, 'Think-it-over Hanratty'. I had Mary Bridget and Gregory and O'Brien. I must pull my weight too . . . work myself into the ground, so that I slept at nights. There would be hard physical labour in plenty, to drive away my pain . . .

The plans churned over in my head till

it was time to go to bed and I was asleep the moment I closed my eyes . . . soon awake again. It may have been a gust of wind that aroused me or flung rain on the pane, but I put out a hand to find Gareth before I remembered it all. I got out of bed and stood, looking down at the silver path of the moon across the sea. I wondered where Gareth was in the great silence of the universe and if he could see me where I stood, lonely for him. Then I thought of the baby and the clothes I must find . . . the wallpaper for his room, his cot. Thank God I was not in need or in sickness . . . only in sorrow. Cool-na-Grena would be my monument for Gareth. I was glad suddenly that I was going to bring his things over . . . his desk, his paintings, his car. If I could not bring myself to talk about him and live with the things he had known, I would shut him out from this peaceful place . . .

I woke in the morning to find O'Brien at my bed, planning whether the baby's wallpaper should be trains or dolls.

"It will have to be a-sexual, Lalage. You'd go and have a girl to spite me if

I picked the trains."

I got out of bed and went to brush my hair.

"You might have twins under that nightdress and never know it even at full term," she declared. "It's like a ball gown."

I ignored her compliment and turned back to the wallpaper.

"Nursery rhymes or Micky Mouse or that sort of motif," I suggested. "But there's all the layette to be thought of too."

"I've got a book about baby clothes in my luggage somewhere," she exclaimed. "I'll go and root it out and we'll make out a list of what's necessary."

She went off to her room and I crossed to the wash-hand stand to fetch my toilet things, for it was time I was getting along to the bathroom. My pink toothbrush was set out on the top ledge, but somebody had left a green one by the side of it. I turned on my heel and went back across the room, my hand against my breast, and I felt like an old, old woman. The familiar agony was back in full force in the roots of my tongue and down into my throat. I heard O'Brien open the door and I knew she would see something was wrong.

"I'm sorry," I whispered and my voice was breaking. "I don't seem to be able to help it. It's one of the little things. The toothbrush just now . . . I don't know how I can be so vulnerable about such a small thing. It's stupid when you come to think of it . . . "

I sat there looking down at the green toothbrush, clasped in my hand still.

"Just because for three years and three months, twice in every day, I put an inch of paste on a green toothbrush and then on a pink one, why can I feel such agony? Is it going to be like this for ever, for if it is, I can't bear it. Oh, God! He used to use mine sometimes to tease me. He was always playing tricks on me. Once he put some cold cream on my toothbrush for fun, when we were going out to dinner. I saw him do it and I changed it over to his. He watched me brushing my teeth and couldn't understand what had gone amiss, till he did his own teeth. He had his dress shirt on. I can see him now, as clearly as I see you. How can I face it that it's over for ever . . . all that laughter and happiness? I'll stop brushing my teeth if I can't stop being such a baby."

"I shouldn't do that, Mrs Kingston. They're very nice teeth."

I was horrified to hear Gregory's voice. I sat up with a jerk and met his eyes in the mirror. Thank the Lord I was not weeping, but I was marooned out there by the dressing table in my nightdress, with no hope of bolting back across the room to my bed.

"You're not a baby," he said, putting down a tray he was carrying and picking up my dressing gown from the end of the bed. He came across and helped me shrug my shoulders into it and he showed no embarrassment at finding me in such a predicament.

"You didn't answer when I knocked at the door. I thought you'd gone along to the bath. I brought up your tea to save Hannah's legs on the stairs. Would you like to get back to bed and have it in comfort?"

I tightened the sash of my dressing gown and went over to climb into bed again.

"I suppose you heard all about the toothbrush," I muttered, and he nodded his head, his eyes very sad.

"I thought it was O'Brien. She went to fetch a book for me. I'm sorry to have made such an exhibition of myself . . . "

He gave me my tea on the small silver tray and then went to stand by the door, his hand on the knob, his face troubled.

"I wonder if you'd believe me if I told you three facts, that I've personally proved to be true?"

I concentrated all my attention on my tea and could think of nothing to say to him and after a little pause, he went on in rather an uncertain voice.

"Time takes the sting out of that kind of thing . . . the torment of memory. That's the first truth. The second is that hard work has the same effect . . . really hard work, mental or physical, so that when you go to bed, you sleep . . . "

"And the third thing?" I prompted him for he said no more and I was thinking that this was a strangely philosophical man to be a farm steward.

"There's a magic about Cool-na-Grena," he said. "It's nothing one can analyse, or write down, or put a finger on, but it's real. Cool-na-Grena does something to every single person who comes to live here. There's a 'balm of hurt minds' to be found here."

So he knew his Shakespeare, I thought, and he was a man who had known adversity too. I could sense a mystery about him and one day, I might solve it. I thanked him and promised to think over what he had just told me and I tried to express my gratitude for the way they had all helped me. I would get up and have my bath now and after breakfast, we could do our proposed inspection of the property.

After breakfast, I found that my retinue of the day before had formed in the hall. Mary Bridget had added a pair of man's Wellington boots to her pink housemaid's uniform, that did nothing to improve her appearance. I asked to see the garden first, so we went out by the back door, down a small flight of steps with an iron hand-rail.

The fowls were free to wander where they pleased in the yard and orchard and they had turned the whole place into a grey no-man's-land of smooth earth, interspersed with hollows, that they had scratched out. It gave the back premises an untidy uncared-for appearance and I decided that they must be put into a concentration camp forthwith. The henhouse had been fashioned from tree trunks and roofed in with bracken and I did not blame the birds for preferring to roost in the trees, for the roof had caved in and the walls were leaning every way.

"A new hen-house and a few hundred feet of wire for a run . . . " I said. "I seem to remember that the wire must be six feet high."

Mary Bridget agreed with this at once.

"That's true, Ma'am," she said. "The old cock can fly like an aigle and he after the hens."

I told her that, in future, I wanted to put her in charge of some of the out-door things, the hens, the garden, a few ducks and turkeys perhaps . . . a pig or two, and her whole face lit up.

"Oh, Ma'am!" she sighed.

"We'll have to look out for somebody to take your place in the house."

Hannah folded her arms on her bosom at that.

"If old 'Think-it-over' Hanratty would let the girl get married, we'd have a fellow worth four of these young girls in the house," she declared.

Mary Bridget got very red at that and scuffed in the dust with the toe of her Wellington, while Hannah went on to explain that she was walking out with a boy called John-Joe, who didn't come up to the top of her ear. John-Joe worked for Molloy, the contractor, and it was a crying shame to have him digging ditches, when he could make an omelette, that would coax the birds down out of the trees.

"He can do any mortal thing in a house," she went on. "Twig the carpets, scrub the floors. You should see the shine he puts on the brasses, the night he comes to call for Mary Bridget. He polished the lamp in the dining room, specially for Mr Gregory last week and it was like the day it came out of the shop."

"And Mary Bridget's father does not approve as much as you, Hannah?"

"He says John-Joe doesn't make enough to keep a pig," Mary Bridget whispered and I told her that if he came to live in, that would be changed.

"You couldn't afford it, Ma'am," she worried. "I don't want you in the workhouse, along of John-Joe and me."

I did nothing to dispel the illusion of my poverty, for money has a way of destroying precious things, things such as I had found in this valley. I did not want my magic to vanish, so I kept my own council, as we went into the garden by the Gothic gate. There had been box edging, but it had shot up nine feet in the air to rival the unpruned fruit trees and rampant fuchsia bushes. There were roses struggling against neglect, filling the garden with scent and I gathered an armful of them. In the greenhouse, which had very little glass intact, there were tomatoes.

"I'll bring out a basket and pick some of these. We'll have tomato soup for dinner and I'll make some chutney out of the unripe ones . . . and look at those Conference pears. Are there any Kilner jars in the pantry, Hannah? I could try my hand at bottling them."

She shook her head, but she was pleased at my enthusiasm.

"We'll buy some in Cork, when we go in," I planned. "I must get a butcher's apron too to save my clothes. That's far better than any fancy apron you can buy anywhere, but there's so much to do out here."

"If we had John-Joe Foley for the house, Mary Bridget and I would soon get the land into shape," said Gregory.

We walked the sloping gentle hills, till we came to the head of the waterfall, with the grass springy beneath our feet. The air was filled with the heavy scent of the gorse. The dam was directing a long skein of white wool into the pool below and there was a haze of spray above it. It was my rainbow glass again. I remembered the wedge of glass my father had had and how he had let me look through its prism into fairyland. I looked through the rainbow glass of the spray now and saw the old house in the valley, all red, orange, yellow, green, blue, indigo and violet. It was beautiful, remote, calm . . . and my ears were filled with the sweet sounds of the murmuring bees and the running water.

Perhaps I had wandered into a land of enchantment, where I might find peace and happiness, I thought, and then I remembered that my father was gone and the rainbow glass lost for ever and that happiness was not for me. I forced myself back to the present and went quickly down to the drive . . . forced myself to discuss how we must spread gravel there . . . and knew the gravel would be no harder than the stone that was my heart.

"It'll take time . . . so much time . . . so much to do. We'll have to cut the trees on the avenue back too," I sighed.

At that, O'Brien tucked her arm in mine and laughed.

"Sure, haven't we all the time in the world, honey?"

I thought bitterly that I had far too much of it. Then I forced my mind away from sadness and listened to Gregory discussing the barn. We had inspected it earlier on and found that it was a lean-to-shed on the tall wall of the enclosed garden. It had been divided up into four sections, each about twelve feet by ten. The roof of bracken had caved in, but Gregory had plans for it.

"The timber is as sound as the day it was built, Mrs Kingston, uprights, rafters, doors and everything else. It only wants a new roof of good strong galvanised iron and it would house Mary Bridget's pigs and perhaps a cow or two as well."

"Will we put the galvanised iron on the shopping list too, Gregory?" O'Brien teased him, and I shook my head and murmured "Festina lente," and was surprised when he looked over at me gravely.

"All the same, Mrs Kingston, we mustn't go too slowly. We can't leave that barn much longer, if we want to have it finished before the winter storms."

We walked out along the springy grass to the point and as we had already explored the sandy beach, we went down the steps on the right, where the shore was rocky as far as the next headland. The steps were of railway sleepers and had been freshly repaired. As we came down to the sea level, I heard Gregory's voice at my back.

"There's a reef, that runs out to that island. It's dangerous to swim off the point for it's full of currents. When it's calm, the sandy bay is quite pleasant, but if you want deep water, you've got it here."

I let him come past me and followed him round a shoulder of the cliff and there was a natural pool in the rocks, that was far better than any swimming bath I had ever seen. It would wash right over with the sea at high tide and there were steps cut out in the side of it, so that it would be easy to walk down into the water, if one did not want to dive in.

"Mr Gregory cut the steps specially for you," Hannah told me, and he frowned at her, as if he did not want me to know it. "He thought it might be hard for you to come up out of the pool without them, but it's not deep at this end. It's well over your head at the far side. You'd want to take care not to go drowning yourself."

Round another shoulder, we came on a small harbour, that ran back into the land . . . a small natural basin with a concrete slipway in bad repair, and a stone boat-house, just short of derelict, its galvanized roof almost rusted away. There were lobster pots inside, fishing gear too, a pair of oars, a few petrol tins, an outboard motor. Floating in the water was a dinghy and somebody had certainly put in some work on it. It was freshly painted and the brass fittings gleamed . . . the ropes as white as only a seaman could make them. At each side of her bows and across the stern she bore her name. . . *Lalage*, and underneath the name on the stern was painted COOL-NA-GRENA.

"Your work, Gregory?" I asked him and he squatted down to fiddle with the mooring rope after a brief nod.

"We re-christened her," he said, not looking at me. "She was called *Doris*. It was rather apt in view of her new owner."

He was laughing at himself in the strange secret way he had and he had thought that I would not recognise Coleridge, but I was one too good for him there.

"Call me Sappho, call me Chloris, call

me Lalage or Doris . . . Only call me thine . . . " I thought, but I said nothing. Gregory was ex-British navy in the cut of his jib and I would solve that mystery in my own time, but now I had a sailor, who quoted Coleridge and Shakespeare and had known what I meant when I said "Festina lente."

"You certainly made a good job of her," I murmured. "And of the pool too. You seem to have been working very hard on my behalf, one way and another."

It was close on lunch-time when we got back to the house and I had collected a bit of old wire netting on the way. With two bowls and the wire and the roses, between us all, we managed two very professional flower arrangements, one for the hall and one for a low table in the sitting room, and the old house seemed to turn over in its sleep and sigh.

In the afternoon, O'Brien and I took the car down to the cross-roads to Mr Slattery's shop, where there was an Aladdin's cave of goods . . . scrubbing brushes, hot water bottles, sides of bacon, balls of string, spades, bags of Indian meal for the hens, Kilner jars, pickling spice, hen wire, butter, salt, tea, sugar . . . Mr Slattery was the most friendly and obliging shop-keeper I had ever met. He promised to 'run our purchases up to the house' and he even lent us a heavy mallet to drive in the stakes for the poultry run. He sent his daughter off post haste to a farm near by and she was back in a short while, with a chicken all trussed up and oven ready . . . and a jug of fresh cream.

There was such a friendly atmosphere about the shop . . . such a personal element, that I found it delightful after the tumble of shopping in town. Mr Slattery came out on the road to wave farewell to us and wish us safe home.

Back at Cool-na-Grena, O'Brien and Gregory set about getting the sitting room cleared for its decorating. Mary Bridget went off to get the hen run ready for the wire and Hannah and I had a wonderful time in the kitchen, which she enjoyed as much as I.

That night we supped royally from tomato soup, roast chicken and trifle. Then Gregory, O'Brien and I . . . joined later by Hannah and Mary Bridget sat round the desk in the morning room and made plans. There was to be a shopping expedition the next day to the City of Cork. We made plans for the restoration of Cool-na-Grena and we built some very fine castles in the air . . . castles as fine as any I had ever seen in my rainbow glass.

4

I Meet 'Think-It-Over' And John-Joe

THE drive to Cork was over in a flash, because O'Brien and I had so much to discuss. We talked about vests and shawls and cots and baths and prams . . . of daffodil bulbs and wallflowers and how I must rescue the ornamental urns, that were being used for drinking troughs for the hens and get them painted and positioned one each side of the front steps. We talked of bottling apple pulp and making blackberry jam . . . of interior decoration and tiling, of the choice of thick paper in French grey, which would go with anything, for the sitting room and the staircase and probably the dining room too. Then we were in the city and the shops were spreading their goods out to tempt us. The assistants were piling some of their wares into the boot of the car. It was well after lunch time, when we were suddenly exhausted and O'Brien drove the car towards home and stopped on the way by a sandy bay to eat our picnic. Apropos of nothing, she turned the subject to Gregory, who was at Cool-na-Grena seeing to the burning of the worm-riddled furniture of the morning room.

"Gregory's a dark horse," she exclaimed. "I know you told me that your cousin took him on before the accident. I know that your cousin was in the Navy Volunteer Reserve and that he was in that rescue operation on the burning pier, but where does Gregory come in? He's got a past and he's hiding out from something. I wonder if he was involved with the accident."

I told her I knew very little about it. Dermot had been sheltering under a tree and had been killed by lightning. I had not liked to talk to Hannah about it, for she had been very attached to Cousin Dermot.

"Gregory's a man of mystery," O'Brien assured me. "I heard Mary Bridget telling Hannah that he was 'on the run' yesterday . . . and there is something very queer about him. I noticed it as he came up the side of the waterfall. Do you know what he was wearing?"

"A pair of slacks and a seaman's sweater," I answered and took a bite from a chicken and ham sandwich, crisp with our home-grown lettuce, that we had found in the garden. "There's nothing mysterious about that. The house is by the sea. He'd been working on the dinghy."

"On his hand," she said patiently. "What was he wearing on his hand?"

I confessed myself ignorant, so she told me and I was so surprised that I almost choked myself.

"He had a twin of your husband's signet ring on the little finger of his left hand . . . same crest and all."

"You must have imagined it."

"It was the same double eagle. Besides, I've seen it since. Maybe he stole it."

"He wouldn't steal," I murmured. "You must have been mistaken."

"He wore it again that night at supper, but he hasn't had it on since. I expect he saw the duplicate on your hand and thought you'd notice it."

"He wouldn't steal . . . " I said and she agreed with that.

"Maybe he's an O'Connell Kingston," she suggested. "He might be an illegitimate son or something like that. They all know about it but only us two. I didn't like to speak to you, till we were out of the house on our own, for there's a conspiracy of secrets, that you could cut with a knife."

"And now, maybe you'll solve it?" I suggested and she said she'd lay a bet with me that she'd have the answer by Christmas.

I had a suspicion that she was just trying to cheer me up and that she had made up the whole thing.

"If you solve it before Christmas, O'Brien, I'll give you an ostrich feather hat and a pair of golden slippers that will never wear out."

"Jesus, Mary and Joseph! Won't I be a sight for sore eyes?" she exclaimed. "And suppose I lose?"

I grinned at her and knew that I loved her more than any sister. She had never failed to chase away the black dog from my shoulder.

"You can rebuild the boathouse down on the shore and paint the roof of it in any colour I choose . . . and I'll take my time about choosing it too, for you'll not find the answer to Gregory. He's a deep, dark, silent one."

She tidied up the picnic things and flung half a sandwich to a swooping gull. Then we set out for home. She did not speak till we came in sight of the gates, but she was turning the conversation over in her mind.

"You're a deep, dark, silent one yourself, Lalage," she laughed. "And there's our man, down the road a piece, waiting for us . . . and I'll start my investigation straight away."

He came over to smile at us through the open window and told us that he was on his way back from Hanratty's cottage. The old man would call to see me in the morning. I worried a little that there was no room in the car for us to offer him a lift, but O'Brien was out of her seat in a flash and was telling him she would walk up the drive with him . . . giving me a wink behind his back. As I drove off, I heard her opening shot . . .

"Wasn't Mrs Kingston's cousin struck by lightning under one of these trees?"

They had not been idle in our absence. The sitting room was ready for papering. Some of the hens' wire was up. The worm-eaten furniture was a pile of grey ash.

I went to bed early that night and did not dream. I suffered from my dreams as much as anything else. They were happy sometimes, so that when I woke, like Caliban, I wept to sleep again . . . but there were times, when I had fearsome nightmares, full of graves and coffins and I ran and ran and could not escape from them, woke up sweating with terror, and found only desolation in being alone.

Before breakfast, O'Brien came into my room to tell me that Gregory was a close one, as if I had not told her the same thing the afternoon before.

"He was at sea in the war. That's why Dermot took him on here. That's all I found out . . . "

I interviewed old Hanratty in the morning room after we had finished breakfast. He was a saintly looking man, with a shining bald dome of a head, that had retained just a fringe of longish white silky hair. He had a bristling walrus moustache and bristling eyebrows to match it, and little twinkling blue eyes.

"I'm glad to make your acquaintance," I began formally. "I wanted to talk to you about Mary Bridget. I've been very pleased with her work here and I was thinking of moving her out to take charge of the garden and the fowls and that type of thing, but I thought I had better ask your advice, first of all."

He was inclined to be shy with me and to twiddle his cap round in his hands, but I got him to sit down on a chair opposite mine and he perched on the edge of it, like an elderly uncomfortable bird.

"'Tis a fine morning, Ma'am," he remarked. "Glory be to God!"

I saw I was being far too un-Irish. I moved my ideas over the sea to Argyll and imagined that I was back at home in the old house and had never lived in the rat-race of a great modern city. Old Hanratty and I discussed Scotland for five minutes and how like it was to Ireland. Then we talked of planes and flying and how a person could flit from one country to another almost in the twinkling of an eye. We came by easier stages to Ballyboy and Mr Slattery at the Cross Roads Stores and 'Think-it-over' told me that Mr Slattery was a decent man, who wouldn't cut your throat for sixpence. We arrived at the subject of Mary Bridget in a very gracious and pleasant manner and he told me that she was the equal of two good men on the land and that I showed grand judgement.

"I'd be glad of your help too," I said. "Mary Bridget was sure you'd come and do some work for me. I hope you will."

"It would be an honour to work in Cool-na-Grena again," he said simply. "Many's the time I've worked here in the old days, and a lovely house it was then . . . aye and will be again, with yourself and Mr Gregory to put it where it stood before . . . "

"Mr Gregory . . . " I echoed and there was a change of expression in his face . . . a kind of watchfulness, a guarding.

"He told me all you want done, Ma'am . . . the kitchen floor down first, then the water heating . . . the sink in the kitchen, the new baths and the general plumbing. He said you'd like a small bathroom to yourself in the old Master's dressing room, and sure, nothing would be easier. Aren't the two rooms back to back? 'Twould be nothing more than the cost of the bath and the bowl and the lavatory pan. Did Mr Gregory tell you about the Colonel's stove?"

It appeared that 'the Colonel' had recently had oil-fired central heating installed and his old solid fuel stove was redundant. He had given it to 'Think-it-over' to take away and it was at the moment reclining in his shed. 'I could have it and welcome' and it would cost me what it had cost him and that was nothing. It was powerful enough to take central heating in Cool-na-Grena, if ever I wanted it.

Finally we went on a tour of the house and spent the most enjoyable morning over it and then I invited him to take lunch with Mary Bridget and he accepted my invitation with dignity and grace. At this point, I pretended to remember something else I wanted to discuss with him and took him back to the morning room.

"I wonder if you'd be able to advise me about a man, I'm thinking of taking on to work in the house. You must know all the local people. This boy's name is Foley."

"John-Joe Foley?" he asked and I nodded.

"He's got good recommendations," I went on. "I want him to replace Mary Bridget at the inside work. He'd have to do all the usual things a house-boy does . . . work in the kitchen, answer the door, that sort of thing. He'd live in and I'd pay him so much a week."

Here I mentioned a sum well in excess of what John-Joe got from Molloy, the contractor. I had been doing some research with Mary Bridget on this point and I tossed out the information lightly and passed on in a most casual manner, or so I hoped.

"Unfortunately he's not married. I'd have preferred a married man, but apparently his girl's father won't hear of marriage till he gets a better job. What do you think about him? If you say he'd be suitable, I'll give him the position."

"Let me think it over," he said and went to look out through the window for two minutes, after which he turned back into the room and searched my face with his eyes.

"Do you know that he's walking out with Mary Bridget?" he asked me point-blank, but I sidestepped the question.

"Your Mary Bridget! Our Mary Bridget? Why then, that's wonderful. You've solved all my problems for me. If that's the case, I know he'd be very suitable indeed. Of course, you won't refuse your consent any longer. You know I'll treat them fairly . . ."

We settled Mary Bridget's affairs to our mutual satisfaction and he took himself off to the kitchen, but he had not been gone thirty seconds, when the lady herself came creeping into the room like a mouse.

"John-Joe is below in the pantry," she whispered. "He came to see you, but the old fellow was here, so I had to hide him. I'll bring him out as soon as the Da is off the premises. Is he going to do the floor for us?"

I told her we were to have a new floor

and a new sink and hot and cold running water, but she was not interested, though she pretended to be, out of politeness. She was bursting to find out if I had asked her father about John-Joe and herself, but I knew it must be John-Joe's privilege to give her the joyful news for himself.

"Has John-Joe ever proposed to you in so many words?" I asked her and she got very red and stood over by the door, wringing out the pink dishcloths, for the topic was a delicate one.

"Arrah, he has and he hasn't, Ma'am."

"It wouldn't do if your father was to say 'yes' and John-Joe was to say 'no'," I pointed out. "You'd better send him in to me and come back yourself in a little while. I'll have the situation clarified by then."

"What does that mean?" she asked me, her hand at her lips and her face full of apprehension.

I smiled at her and told her I wanted to get the whole matter straightened out and she looked miserable.

"You mightn't like him, Ma'am. He's not very big."

"I don't think that'll worry me . . . and incidentally, I hope that you'll see to it that he gets his lunch."

She grinned at that and I loved her for her simplicity.

"Ach, sure, won't he have the half of mine?"

He might have been a Spaniard or a southern Italian by the darkness of his skin, and his hair was straight and as jet black as an Indian's, his eyes liquid brown. He was short and slight in stature and he had a gentle way with him and a soft kindness in his voice, that made me like him from the start. He worshipped Mary Bridget, to whom we referred throughout the interview as Miss Hanratty. At first, I did not realise whom he meant and thought he must have another sweetheart. Then I saw it was his genteel way of speaking, for John-Joe was nothing, if he was not genteel. Most definitely, he told me he had proposed to Miss Hanratty, but 'she had his heart scalded with her flighty ways'. He had been proposing to her for six years, but 'her old divil of a father' was against the match. When I told him that this was no longer the case, he was full of gratitude to me and I quickly changed the subject by telling about the position I wanted him to fill. I gave him details of the work and the wages and the holidays and he looked at me in surprise.

"I wouldn't want holidays, nor time off neither in a place like this . . . not married to Miss Hanratty and all."

I heard Miss Hanratty's hand on the door knob and stood up. We shook hands on our bargain and I wished him every success in his new work and hoped that his marriage would bring him great happiness. Mary Bridget came in then and I told her that I approved of her choice very much and went quickly out of the room and left them alone. I was angry with myself to find my eyes full of tears, for I thought how they walked in the Garden of Eden . . . and I had been shut out of mine for ever. I opened the front door and stood looking down on the Atlantic, with the tears misting the light from the water and the sky into a dazzle of brightness. Then I heard Gregory's steps come walking up the hall at my back and I put out my hands to the sides of the doorway, so that he should not come past and see my face.

"I've engaged John-Joe," I told him, when he stopped behind me. "I think he'll fit in very well . . ."

I put up a hand and brushed my left cheek casually, and he said nothing, so I went on again.

"Mary Bridget will be a kind of land-girl. I'll get her some buff-coloured smocks and we'll tidy her hair into a neat pony tail. You won't know her."

"She won't know herself," he laughed. "She'll be delighted to get shut of the housework and to marry John-Joe . . . all this and heaven too."

I brushed my right cheek quickly.

"John-Joe can take over her work in the house. You'll still have to supervise the whole place, of course, but we'll tackle the garden between us, Mary Bridget and you and I. That garden wall will have to be rebuilt and it will be tough going."

"We'll rebuild it," he said quietly and I got out my handkerchief and blew my nose and felt ready to turn round and face him at last.

"I won't be able to help much soon, at

least not with the heavy work. I'll do the best I can, while I can. After the baby's born, then I'll really be able to pull my weight . . . "

He glanced at my face for a moment and then looked past me down to the sea, while I sighed that it would be months before we were straight, but that I did not care about that, for I had a dreadful lot of time to fill in.

He looked at me again at that and told me that nobody knew how much time there was left to them and he was mighty serious all of a sudden.

"Dermot thought he had a lot of time to fill in," he said. "And he was gone between one day and the next."

"Did you know him well?" I asked and his eyes were troubled. He avoided the question too.

"I wasn't here very long, before the accident, Mrs Kingston."

I held my hand out to him with the ring crest-uppermost.

"Did he wear a ring like mine?"

He took my hand in his and bent his head down to look at the ring closely and

I could no longer see the expression on his face.

"He had one just like it. It was on his hand the evening he was killed."

"Do you know what's become of it?"

He was awkward all at once, as if he were guilty, yet somehow not guilty too and he covered the situation with a smoke screen of vagueness.

"It'll be in the house somewhere. All his effects have been left exactly as they were, till you said what you wanted done with them. I'll look out the ring for you, if you like."

"There's no hurry about it. I never met Dermot, you know. What was he like?"

"About my height and build, dark too. He was a fine man. He'd broken his heart over Cool-na-Grena and the state it was in. He loved Cool-na-Grena."

"He'd broken his heart over a dead phoenix?" I put in. "Wasn't that a bit foolish of him? The phoenix never dies."

"'Resurgam'," he said. "That was on the scroll of the ring. I must try and find it for you . . ."

I walked past him and went up the stairs and he looked up at me through the wrought iron banisters.

"It's no disgrace to weep, when your heart is broken," he said in such a low voice, that I wondered if I had heard him aright. Then I remembered Cousin Dermot and halted on the stairs.

"Was Dermot weeping over Cool-na-Grena?" I asked him.

"It wasn't Dermot I meant, Mrs Kingston," he said and went off along the hall to the kitchen without another word.

I climbed the rest of the stairs slowly and my hand was on the door to my room, when I thought that the door across the landing moved. It was Dermot's old room and a twin of my own and the door was ajar. As I pushed it open and walked in, the smell of must and disuse came out to meet me. The curtains were drawn across the two windows, as if Dermot still lay dead in the house. I pulled them back and let the sunshine stream in on the solid Victorian furniture . . . wardrobe, chest of drawers, wash-hand stand, dressing table, bed, desk. The desk was far too good to be hidden away up here and I determined to have it in the sitting room, as soon as things were straight. I lifted back the top of it and saw the papers and letters in the pigeon holes, just as he had left them. I shivered and went across to the wardrobe to swing the doors open and all the time I felt as if somebody was watching me. The wardrobe was divided into two sections, one for hanging and the other with shelves, that pulled out. His suits were there and a tweed overcoat with raglan sleeves, a navy gaberdine raincoat and the black uniform of a Lieutenant in the Royal Naval Volunteer Reserve. I drew the shelves out, one after the other, and saw the shirts and underclothes, the white polo-necked sweater, some ties and socks. On the bottom shelf was a folded naval greatcoat with the uniform cap laid on top of it. I closed the doors again and went over to the dressing table in the far window. The things, that had stood on top of it, had been tidied away into the centre drawer . . . a yellowish-white comb, two silver-backed brushes, a bottle of brilliantine, a box of studs. The brushes were monogrammed D.O'C.K. and there were hairs caught in the bristles, the same dark hair that Gregory had. I unscrewed the nozzle of the brilliantine bottle and shook out a drop of it into my hand and it had a vague scent, which reminded me, sharply and nostalgically of my dead father . . . a smell of bay rum, and leather and shaving soap.

There was shaving tackle still set out on the wash-hand stand, a toothbrush and paste, a tablet of soap, all waiting for Dermot O'Connell Kingston to use again. It was as if all these inert things knew that he was not dead . . . as if they waited for him to come walking into the room again. I got a prickling sensation in the nape of my neck and again, the door seemed to move a little, as if somebody had put a hand on the panel. I ran quickly across and flung it open, but there was nobody there . . . only the scent of his brilliantine from my hand, and the wind laughing in the chimney at my foolish fancy, that for a moment, Dermot himself had stood there and put out his hand and touched the panel of the door.

I went back to the bed and opened the drawer of the bedside table and there was a Bible there, very old and battered. I picked it up and opened it at the fly-leaf, read the copper-plate writing . . .

Dermot O'Connell Kingston,
Cool-na-Grena,
Ballyboy,
Co. Cork,
Ireland,
The British Isles,
Europe,
The World,
The Universe,
Space . . .

IF THIS BOOK SHOULD CHANCE TO ROAM
BOX ITS EARS AND SEND IT HOME.

I turned the leaves over idly and a coloured text fell out, the sort that are handed out to the children in Sunday School. I picked it up from where it had fallen on the floor and looked at it. There was a picture of a shepherd on it, with a lamb across his shoulders and around it was written, "Yea, though I walk through the Valley of the Shadow of Death, I shall fear no evil, for Thou art with me."

Poor Dermot had gone through the valley of the shadow. I hoped that there had been no time for him to fear terror. I flicked the pages of the Bible over and came on a photograph, post-card size, of a boy in school uniform. I was startled to see that it might have been Gregory as a boy, for it bore a marked resemblance to him. The boy looked big-eyed and uncomfortably starchy in a high Eton collar with a vista of palm trees at his back. On the back of it, pencilled very faintly was written 'Dermot, aged 12 years'.

I hurried across the landing to my own room and shut the door behind me, sat down on the bed, with my heart beating fast. It was impossible that Gregory should be Dermot O'Connell Kingston, or was it? There was all this mystery about him, and O'Brien had said he wore the phoenix ring. But why should he pretend to be dead? They would all have to be in the plot, Hannah, Mary Bridget, old Hanratty and John-Joe. It was quite impossible, yet I must get to the bottom of Gregory's mystery. If there was a conspiracy of silence . . . a chain of people all with a secret, I asked myself which was the weakest link and I knew at once that Mary Bridget was the person to tackle. I would spend the afternoon tidying the flower beds in front of the house and I would ask Mary Bridget to help me.

After lunch therefore, I put my plan into operation and very pleasant work it was. There was a light wind, blowing in from the Atlantic and the air was like champagne.

The four crescentic beds were arranged round the sweep of the drive and she and I worked our way through them companionably, side by side. It was wonderful how quickly we got the place looking better.

"Did my Cousin Dermot ever do any gardening?" I asked her after a while.

"He didn't bother with the flowers, Ma'am. He might do a bit in the vegetable garden, if he had to, but he didn't like it."

"Who did the flower garden then?"

"Old Mrs Kingston kept it lovely when she was alive. I wasn't here then, but Hannah would tell you. When she died, nobody touched it at all, till I came. I used to do it an odd time, but Mr Dermot didn't care about it. He hadn't the heart for anything."

"It was a strange way to die," I remarked carelessly and she nodded her head in agreement.

"You can say that again, Ma'am. It wouldn't happen again in a thousand years."

"They say lightning never strikes twice in the same place. I suppose it could never happen again."

"I can't understand how he was so foolish as to stand under a tree and the storm on. He knew it was dead too and that it would come down as easy as wink. Sure, a push would have put it over."

"Was he killed by the tree then? Or was he struck by lightning?"

"Ah, you wouldn't know. He was that disfigured. Hannah said he was crushed like a beetle, that you'd put your foot on . . . "

She had the peasant love of tragedy and drama.

"It was the day the queer fella come. I was feeding the hens, and he come round the corner of the house and frightened the wits out of me. He was a tough looking fella and I thought he was one of the fishermen, come about the old boat. I gave him a cup of tea in the kitchen and then Mr Dermot come back and gave him a drink and some clothes. It was when he was seeing him off at the front gate, that it happened. Poor Mr Dermot! Always as brave as a lion. I wonder would the fear have come upon him, if he could have seen the death he was to have . . . "

I was wondering if my unborn infant would ever inherit Cool-na-Grena after all. There seemed to be a possibility that Dermot O'Connell Kingston was in the sitting room at that very moment, papering the walls and listening to O'Brien's laughter. I would find it all out in time and there was no hurry. I was quite confident that Gregory would never do anything mean or dastardly. If he had broken the law, it was because the law was unfair. He was no criminal and he meant me no evil. It would all work out in the end and I had all the time in the world to finish the jig-saw puzzle. I thought of the slow march of the hours and put my hand on the pedestal of stone in the centre of the circular sweep.

"There should be a sun dial for the top of this, Mary Bridget."

She wiped her hands down the sides of her dress and told me it was propping the pantry window open and she ran off through the door and was back presently with John-Joe by her side. He had moved in straight away, she told me, in case I changed my mind. Together we fitted the sun dial in position and it shone like a small sun, for John-Joe had polished it before they brought it out to me.

TEMPORA MUTANTUR ET NOS
MUTAMUR IN ILLIS.

"Times change and we change with them," I murmured almost to myself and John-Joe said that was a true word, for whoever had written it.

"Sure the Angel of the Lord couldn't have brought more change for the better into my life, Ma'am, and I thank you kindly."

I was embarrassed by his gratitude and

sent him in to fetch the others out to look at our sun dial and Gregory was every bit a seaman, as he told us we had positioned it incorrectly, and put it to rights himself, with due regard for the compass points. O'Brien was white with fatigue and refused to rest, so I said I wanted fish for breakfast and asked him to take her out in the dinghy to relax over a fishing line for a few hours. They went off together so gaily that I wondered if he was falling in love with her. Then I turned my attention back to the flower beds and as John-Joe stayed to help us, we got them finished in record time. Then we all went off to the kitchen and I turned out a coffee soufflé, that I had made the day before.

I had a most appreciative audience, as I put chopped walnuts round the sides of it. Then John-Joe asked to decorate the top with cherries and angelica and made such a masterpiece of it, that Hannah declared it was too beautiful ever to put a spoon in it.

That afternoon, too, we explored the pantry for hidden treasure and found most of a dinner service in Mason's ironstone china, and silver entrée dishes too, to say nothing of a silver soup tureen with a lid that flipped over. We washed, we polished, we pressed everything into service and that night we produced a supper that was almost perfect. My urge to get the proper equipment for cooking was overcoming my dread of seeing my old things again. I determined to concentrate on the china and the glass, on the pots and the pans, and try to forget the old, hurtful, painful, personal items. I must blot out the memory of Gareth's wardrobe and the double bed with the pink quilted head-board . . . the willow pattern jumbo cup, he had always used at breakfast, the silver tankard.

I was changing into a silk dress for supper, when O'Brien came walking up the path from the point with Gregory at her side and both of them laughing. I watched them from my window and felt shut out and lonely. Again, I wondered if they were falling in love and thought what a suitable match it would be, she, sparkling and vivacious, full of life . . . he, serious and quiet. She was very lovely, seen like that against the sea and the sky. She looked small beside him, yet she was as tall as I was myself. Their dark heads were close together, as they paused to look down at the sun dial and she was telling him a confidence, her lips close to his ear.

I felt the sharp emptiness of loneliness, as I moved away from the window to sit before the dressing table and look at my white miserable face in the glass. My cheeks were hollow and there were big shadows, that had come under my eyes and made them look dark and deep and slanting, the way a hungry cat's eyes might look. My hair was as black as night against the pallor of my face. I put up a hand and lifted it back from my forehead and thought how I had a widow's peak and how apt it was that I had. Then I shook off my self-pity, for the loathsome emotion it was and reached for my dress, to pull it over my head. By the time I was smoothing down the skirt of it, O'Brien was sitting on the foot of the bed, grinning at me.

"You'd want a corkscrew to get a word out of that fellow," she announced. "He knows the whole of my history back to the day the doctor thought I was dead and smacked my little bottom till I took my first breath, but divil a word I got out of him about himself."

"That's too bad," I murmured. "I was thinking of having the boat house roof a dark bottle green colour."

She took no notice of my levity.

"He knows all there is to know about the sea. I found that out, but anyway we knew that already. Still, it was great fun. I don't think I stopped laughing the whole afternoon. Maybe, I'll set my cap at him. It's time I was settling down and he's a handsome bloke. Think of the gorgeous children I'd have from a sire like that."

"I wish you every happiness," I said slyly. "Will you get married in the ostrich feather hat and the golden slippers, or would they be too dressy for Ballyboy Chapel?"

She came over and clutched my arm in mock alarm.

"Give me a day or two, for God's sake. I haven't got as far as that yet."

She walked off to the door at last and stood looking back at me, laughing.

"I didn't waste my time all the same. We caught plenty of mackerel. We could have filled the whole boat with them. He showed me how to do it, with a spool thing trailing behind the back of the boat. He says there's lobsters in the rocks too and if you want some, you've only to ask and he'll catch a few for you. He's very keen to please you."

She closed the door and came back into the room and her voice took on a more confidential note.

"He wanted to know about you . . . all that had happened . . . about your parents and your old home and about Gareth and the flat. He got every single thing I knew about you, out of me. Do you know I think he's struck on you, Lalage? Maybe I'd have my work cut out trying to get him to fall in love with me."

She was only making up all this nonsense to amuse me so I took no notice of her and told her that we would have the mackerel for breakfast.

"There's nothing so delicious as freshly caught mackerel, O'Brien."

She put back her head at that and started to laugh, though I had not the faintest idea what she thought was so funny. She went off to her room at last, still laughing, and at the door, she fired her parting shot.

"I caught more than mackerel this afternoon, Lalage, and that's a fact . . . and by the Holy Fly, it wasn't in the sea, I went fishing!"

5

The Phoenix Begins To Rise

BY October, I was in my fifth month of pregnancy and I had never felt more physically fit, nor had I ever worked harder, but then we all worked hard. By the time each night came, I was so tired that I fell into bed and did not wake till the next morning and my days were too full to find time for weeping.

The running of the house was completely disorganised at first. Mary Bridget, her father and I laid the kitchen floor in one combined operation, while O'Brien and Gregory worked like slaves at the walls of the sitting room, the dining room and the staircase and hall. Hannah and John-Joe coped as best they could with the housework and the cooking and after a time, we began to see the result of our labours. We put tiles round the wall in the kitchen, where the new sink was and where the cooker was to go. I also planned a long working bench under the windows, so we tiled the wall there too.

About this time, I bought a large quantity of galvanised iron from Molloy, the contractor. I saw it lying in his yard one day and asked him about it. It had come from the roof of some big barn they were demolishing and I got it at a fair price. Gregory was very pleased about it, for, as he pointed out, there was so much of it, we could put a fresh roof on our barn and still have plenty over to make a new house for the hens, and it was in excellent condition.

Of course, the reconstruction of the kitchen included the installation of 'the Colonel's' stove. I refused to take this as a gift from 'Think-it-over' and paid him what I thought was a reasonable price for it, but he thought it over a long time indeed, before he would accept it, for he considered it a small fortune. Eventually I had to threaten him that I would employ him no longer if he would not give way to my wishes and then he took the money most reluctantly.

For a few weeks, we lived in a

wilderness of plumbing. There were always pipes being put in there and taken out here, and water being turned off and then turned on again and the taps running . . . to say nothing of baths, basins and lavatory pans, being transported up and down the stairs at all sorts of odd hours.

I took a day off to choose the bathroom suites in Cork city and to fetch the kitchen taps and some other fittings, that were wanted urgently. O'Brien would not come with me. She said she was in some critical stage of papering the upstairs landing, so I asked Gregory if he would accompany me, and left Mary Bridget to help O'Brien. I got an idea that there was a united conspiracy in the household to induce me to take Gregory with me, which I could really not understand. Some days before, I had asked him to sort out Dermot's effects and to take anything he wanted for himself and divide the rest between old Hanratty and John-Joe. I wondered at the time, if it was possible that I was talking to Dermot himself. If the body under the tree had been crushed out of all recognition, I could think of all kinds of fanciful theories of substitution, but none of them seemed very convincing. It was just as possible that Gregory as a boy had had a marked resemblance to Dermot as a boy. At any rate, he thanked me gravely when I asked him to choose what he wanted from Dermot's things. I wanted to go through the desk myself, I told him, but I said nothing about the Bible, which I kept in my bedside table drawer, so that I could study the photograph from time to time and wonder.

He brought the car to the door to collect me and I wondered how he could be so happy about going into Cork, if he were really Dermot. Perhaps he had disguised himself in some way, but that idea was really absurd even to my mind. I had expected him to try to get out of coming with me, but he seemed to be very pleased at the idea. He was wearing a suit of fine hand-woven Irish tweed, which I thought might be one of Dermot's, though it looked as if it had been tailored for himself.

We drove along silently for a while and

then he began to ask me about my old home in Scotland. I could not fathom what interest he could have in the fact that my father had been an expert in the dead languages, but there was no doubt he was. His own father had been a parson, he told me and he had been destined for the same profession. His education at 'R — er-school,' had been classical, with that end in view, but then he had run off to sea and joined the Merchant Navy.

I loved the sea, I said. Our house in Argyll had been on the coast and we had had a launch, rather old and disreputable, and nothing like the dinghy at Cool-na-Grena for spit and polish. I told him how we used to explore the islands of the Hebrides and he said he had been stationed in the Western Isles during the war. He began to talk in a manner that was animated, compared with his usual reticence and I lay back in my seat and listened to him very contentedly.

As we neared Cork, I put out a feeler about Dermot, asked him if he knew anything about the rescue operation and he closed up like a clam at that, but I pursued him with "Had you heard about it?" and then he told me, but he spoke slowly and diffidently now.

"It was in the papers, Mrs Kingston. I read about it. He was in a shore party, that went in to blow up some harbour installations. They were to be taken off by some destroyers, but things got hot. The destroyers were told to return to base. One of them hung about and got the chaps off. That sort of thing was common enough in the war. Do you remember the *Altmark* and 'the Navy's here'?"

His conversation about the *Altmark* was just as animated as his previous talk about the sea. He had steered me away from Cousin Dermot in a very masterly fashion. Yet somehow I sensed that it was a tremendous joke to him and a very private joke too, the way he had managed to turn the topic to a similar but different subject. I got a conviction that he had been personally mixed up with the shore party rescue, for he was the picture of a modest hero, who did not want to discuss his own affairs. There was an air about him that day as if he was learning to laugh again, when he had thought laughter a forgotten pleasure, departed for ever.

Arrived in Cork, we went about our shopping and I chose the two bathroom suites. My bedroom furnishing would be a pink, deep clover, cream motif, so I picked a pink bath for my dressing room, and for the family bathroom I chose primrose. Then we ordered a good cork linoleum in cream for both bathroom floors and for the nursery. In the ironmonger's shop, I tried out a test on him, a masterpiece of espionage to be thought up on the spur of the moment. He was ten yards away from me with his back turned and I picked up a catalogue and called out to him softly.

"Dermot."

He did not move for a full twenty seconds. Then very deliberately he turned round to face me.

"Did you mean me, Mrs Kingston?"

I apologised and told him that Dermot's name must have been in my mind, and he came back to me along the counter, completely unruffled as far as I could see, as I asked his advice about something that I had decided upon already.

When we had concluded all our shopping, he put me into the passenger's seat and grumbled at me that I had made myself far too tired. We drove home companionably silent for the most part and then as we neared Cool-na-Grena again, like Bluebeard's wife, I felt my curiosity get the better of me again.

"It's strange to have inherited a house and never to have met the owner," I remarked. "I know nothing about Dermot, except that he was about your build and dark too . . . and that he was very upset about the state the place was in. Why did he make no effort to do something about it?"

He made me no answer for a very long while and then he glanced at me quickly and away again. I wondered if he was talking about his own trouble, as he told me what had happened.

"Old Mr Kingston let the place get into debt . . . lost all interest when Mrs Kingston died. He drank to forget her. The money went that way. Dermot couldn't get anybody to give him credit . . . couldn't meet the demands, but there was more to it than that . . ."

He paused again, as if he was wondering how much to tell me and I thought that there had been cases before where a person had rigged up the pretence of being dead to collect insurance money . . . to escape from financial tangle. I wondered what he was going to say next, but what he told me was not anything like I expected.

"Dermot had an . . . unfortunate love affair, during the war . . . some girl, who was going to marry him, but . . . didn't. It knocked all the fight out of him. Then the war was over and he came home . . . found the house practically derelict. It was pretty bad trouble . . . "

He seemed to have shrivelled inside and I thought at that moment, that he was surely Dermot. His mind was miles away in space and time and his face was white, his voice inexpressibly sad, as if his heart was breaking all over again with the pain of memory.

"Was he in the Merchant Navy before the war?" I asked him and he turned and looked at me with surprise.

"Good Lord, no! What gave you that idea?"

I had done enough detective work for one day and I spun away to another topic of conversation, but he was sad during the rest of the drive and I was sorry that I had been the cause of his sadness. As we pulled up at the front door of Cool-na-Grena, he turned to me again.

"You should ask Hannah about Dermot. She knows all there is to know about him. She was his nurse from the day he was born and she stayed on as housekeeper, when he grew up and went to school. She worshipped the ground he walked upon."

We went up the steps together and I told him that it only made Hannah sad to talk about Dermot.

"I know she loved him very deeply. It's no good reopening old wounds, is it?"

Then the thought of old wounds made me think of the expected arrival of the furniture from London and I sighed and was every bit as sad as Gregory was himself.

"I wonder when the furniture will arrive," I murmured and was glad when

O'Brien came running down the stairs, her slacks all flecked with white paint, and banished sorrow for both of us by some outrageous remark or another in her usual style.

We had given up all hope of ever seeing the furniture arrive, by the time it came. I stood at one of the sitting room windows, two months later, and watched the sealed vans coming up the drive. An officer had come from the Customs and Excise in Cork and as he went to the back of the first van and broke the seals, I drove my nails into the palms of my hands in an effort not to make a fool of myself. Then I decided that I would not watch it being unloaded. I would walk through the house and see that everything was ready. I went through to the kitchen and looked at the new green tiles on the floor. The steel sink was in use by this time and the chromium taps shone. When I turned on the hot one, the water came out at almost boiling point, for 'Think-it-over' had been right about the capacity of 'the Colonel's' boiler. I examined it now, admiring its black enamel top and its grey mottled sides.

It did its work well and was inexpensive to run.

The two front rooms stood empty to receive the furniture, the paintwork immaculate, the walls elegant . . . but now I could no longer keep away from the windows, but must peer out at the vans outside. The men had unloaded some of the things already. There were rolls of carpet, lying out on the drive, and beside them, the dining room table and chairs. Yet somehow, it did not look like my furniture. I could feel no sorrow in my heart any more, just an emptiness, like hunger, a numbness of feeling, a void. The sea was as grey as a slug, and quiet. The sky was overcast with rain clouds. The persistent rain had swollen the ground to soddenness and it looked as if it would soon rain again. I felt just as sodden with the tears I could not shed, yet I felt no more desire to weep. My breath had fogged the cold pane and I put up a finger to write on the mist . . . GARETH KINGSTON. I felt nothing at all, only an awareness that soon the pain would come shafting through my breast again.

"It's wonderful furniture, Mrs Kingston. O'Brien was quite right about it. It will make a paradise of Cool-na-Grena."

Gregory's voice at my shoulder made me start a little and rub my hand through the words on the glass.

"A paradise?"

My whisper seemed to send its bitterness into every corner of the empty room.

"You don't believe me, do you?" he asked quietly and I turned round slowly and looked up into his face, my lips stiff as I told him that paradise was not for me . . . now or ever.

"Happiness is like the phoenix," he said very gravely and laid his hand down on mine. "It's got the same way of rising from its own ashes. It can be just the same warming comforting flame as it was before."

I shook my head and his grip tightened on my hand.

"I've seen it happen. I promise you. I was so unhappy that I wanted to die . . . and now, I've found myself a corner in the sun, where I'm content . . . all day, every day. It'll be just the same for you. Give it time."

"And is Cool-na-Grena such a paradise for you?" I asked him roughly and he took his hand away at that and walked off from me to the door and I thought he was offended.

"It's an enchanted place. It's as near to paradise as I ever hoped to get."

He was not put out with me, for he swung round all at once and he was laughing, all his seriousness gone in a flash.

"There's a deal of work to be done. I was sent in to station you in the hall to direct the men as they come in through the front door. You'll have to tell them where to put everything. We can't trust anybody else to remember accurately where the stuff's to go . . . "

He made a deprecating moue of his mouth and smiled at me.

"So if you please, we'll leave our discussion of paradise till another time. You'll find out one of these days, that I'm right."

For the rest of that day, I was too busy to marvel at our strange conversation. The operation seemed chaotic and endless, but by dusk, it was over. I watched the empty vans drive off down the avenue and turned to survey my new sitting room, with the blue suite and Dermot's desk, the bookcase, the record-player, the drink cabinet. Even the curtains were up, for Hannah had worked like a slave the whole day to alter all the curtains to fit the windows. I crossed the hall and the dining room had been transformed too. The furniture seemed to bear no resemblance to the things from London. The new setting made it more dignified. The high ceiling gave it an importance I had not thought it possessed before. Perhaps I had become accustomed to a far different standard. At any rate, the whole house was as changed as if some Fairy Godmother had waved her wand over it.

I was exhausted when I went to my room that night and I had been afraid to face the bed with its wine coloured blankets and pink sheets. Yet here the magic had been worked too. The room did not resemble our bedroom at the flat. I went to look out at the cold glimmer of the sea and then turned to admire the Regency wallpaper. There was the familiar dressing table with the plate-glass top and there was my brush and comb set with the petit point backs . . . scent bottles, lipstick, cream jars, lotions and potions. I felt strong and happy, resigned for the first time to my loss of Gareth. I would never look behind me but only to the future. I would find happiness. I went across the carpet and swung back the door of the wardrobe and there was a wide red ribbon that dangled from a hook. There was a Christmas card with a robin . . . on a twig in the snow and a hand-written message in a circle from his mouth.

I LOVE LALLY TOO.

I had not to turn it over to know what was written on the back, only that he loved me for ever. The ribbon fell from my fingers and I thought how awful it was that things survive and people do not. I looked back and was sorry not to turn into a pillar of salt. My pain choked me as I remembered all that was gone and all that would never return again.

6

Surgeon Lieutenant Brendan Barry

WITH all the work in the house, we still had not neglected the yard and garden. We had enclosed the hens in a controlled area and they had a very comfortable house, constructed of posts and galvanised iron. Their nesting boxes were ex-apple boxes from Mr Slattery of the cross-roads and their perches were young saplings culled from the wood. I was allowed the honour of painting the hen establishment and I stood with justifiable pride, spotted from head to foot in blood-red paint and viewed the finished product. Gregory had ploughed up all the back land as far as the garden wall, so it was all neat and tidy.

The flower garden had been left for the present, but we had got the vegetable section whipped into shape and then 'Think-it-over' had turned his attentions to the greenhouse, where he had unearthed a quantity of glass, all ready cut and intact. Somebody must have planned the reconstruction of the glasshouse and then abandoned the work.

"Dermot couldn't have forgotten he had the glass," I said to Gregory, as he painted the finished house one day. "He wouldn't have forgotten an important thing like that."

He looked at me very sadly and remarked that there were some tragedies, which would drive anything out of a person's mind. He finished the work as he spoke and threw the brush back into the paint pot with a sigh.

"Dermot would have been glad to know it was done at last," I said and he looked at me very gravely for a moment before he answered me.

"Perhaps he does know."

I went to work at the flower border, convinced in my mind that he was Dermot, though how he had worked it, I did not know. Perhaps the fisherman called and perhaps he had been killed in the storm. Perhaps identities had been switched. There may have been insurance to be collected. Yet Gregory would never have done anything dishonourable. I gave up thinking about the problem and turned back to the wilderness of thistles and nettles and lupins and foxgloves and delphiniums and verbascums and started to excavate great clumps of the perennials. Later on, Gregory went over the whole area with an auto-cultivator, which he had borrowed from Molloy, the contractor. Then over the next week, the weather was kind and permitted us to get the flowers divided and reset. One day, I was to stand at the iron gate in the high grey-stone wall and exclaim at the glory of the flowers, but that day was not yet. There was the wall itself to build up again in five or six places. There was a strange conversation I had with John-Joe too, when he and I were busy at that same wall.

"You know, Mrs Kingston, you're the spitting image of Mr Dermot's lady."

I took the information as calmly as I could and planted a little house-leek into a crevice of the wall.

"He was engaged to be married, wasn't

he? Why did the girl let him down?"

He stopped up short with a rock in his hand and gazed at me in amazement.

"What in the name of God gave you the idea that Miss Felicity let him down? Did you not know the poor thing was killed in one of them big raids over beyond in England . . . place called Plymouth . . . ?"

I had only to listen. She had been an officer in the W.R.N.S. and she had been engaged to be married. The wedding was but a week off. She had been in an air raid shelter, that had received a direct hit . . .

"She was never found, God rest her. He hadn't even the grave to mourn at. She was a lovely lady. I seen her picture, for he used to carry it with him, everywhere he went. She was the spitting image of yourself, a fine tall girl, with the look of a queen and hair like a raven's wing. Her eyes were as green as the sea . . . Then she was gone and he never got over it . . . came home and found the old place here got to ruin . . . "

I recalled the fisherman and my mind skidded uneasily to one form of disguise and then another . . . a beard perhaps . . . yet a carried photograph might give him away . . .

I shook all nonsense out of my head and turned back to work . . .

* * *

O'Brien had not been neglecting my ante-natal care all these weeks. For all that she was re-decorating the entire house, she kept me firmly under her thumb and made sure that I swallowed my iron and vitamin tablets regularly. No matter what exercise I took outdoors, I still had to perform her 'expectant mothers' physical jerks' twice a day. She was badgering me to see the local doctor too, though so far, I had held out against her on this. She did not like to take complete responsibility for my care, though she was quite capable of it and she begged me to see a Dr Brendan Barry. He was only a young man, she said, but she had found out all about him and he was 'Rotunda-trained'. She said this in a church-service voice and was not amused when I asked her if it meant that he was Court Physician to the Emperor of Ireland. I kept putting her off from one week to the next and made all sorts of excuses, for I was far too busy and felt far too well to see any doctor, and besides, I had complete faith in O'Brien's management. Then one morning, she presented me with a fait accompli. She had telephoned Dr Barry's house the day before and he was visiting me this actual morning. I was to stay in bed till he came.

"I can't stay in bed," I protested. "I'm in the middle of making the hens' drinking troughs with concrete. I'll go to bed when he comes."

"He hasn't the whole day to waste, hanging about the house, waiting for you to come in from the hen run and get yourself washed. You'll stay where you are at this minute and be ready at his convenience."

Of course she got her own way about it. She got her own way about everything.

"It's a funny set-up in Dr Barry's house, Lalage. He has a young one there to take the messages and she'd do far better to be out with a bucket of swill feeding the pigs."

"Oh?" I murmured with an air of polite interest.

"I rang yesterday at nine o'clock sharp and this one answered the phone. Dr Barry couldn't speak to me himself, she said, for he was out on an urgent visit. She'd tell him the minute he got back and he'd be sure to come today."

"That's all right then," I said.

"Indeed and it isn't all right. I asked her if she could give me any idea of the time he'd be calling and she said she couldn't. 'If himself was to be out on a night visit,' she said, 'wouldn't he have to take half the day in bed to recuperate?'"

She drew her dark brows into a frown.

"What's more, Dr Barry was no more out on an urgent case than the tom cat was. I was just going to put down the phone and didn't I hear a voice . . . a man's voice too? It said 'Who the blazes is that at this hour of the day, Bridie?' If I'd been behind him, I'd have given him 'Who the blazes is that?'"

While I was having my bath, she changed all the bed linen, though it had been fresh two days before. Then she put a new tablet of Wright's Coal Tar soap in the bathroom and a spotless linen towel.

"That soap and towel are for the doctor," she cautioned me. "Don't attempt to lay a finger on them."

She put me into my best bed-jacket and lit the electric fire. Then she went downstairs and brought up the bowl of chrysanthemums from the dining room and planked it down on my dressing table. Finally she stood with her hands on her hips and surveyed the whole effect critically.

"You'll do," she said.

I thought that she would do very well herself. She was immaculate in blue dress and white apron. The little American nurses' cap sat jauntily on the back of her glossy head and I thought I had never seen her look so well. I had a scheme afoot to find a husband for her, though she knew nothing about it. I had met nobody I considered suitable for her as yet, only Gregory. If I could get her safely married to some young man in the vicinity, I could ensure that she stayed in County Cork. I could not bear the thought of her being so far from Cool-na-Grena as London, but eligible young men were a scarce commodity in Ballyboy.

Today, I was not even allowed to get up and come down for breakfast. Gregory came up with my tray, because of some affair of estate management he wanted to discuss with me, that could not wait. When we had finished our talk, I grumbled about being kept in bed.

"It's such a waste of time, Gregory. You know I was all ready to fix the troughs for the hens, and here I am, bone idle, while you're all working yourselves to death on my behalf."

He stood at the foot of the bed and smiled down at me.

"Don't you realise that you're doing the most important work of any of us?"

"Having a baby isn't work these days," O'Brien snorted. "It's as easy as falling off a log. You go off about your business, Master Gregory, and get John-Joe to put on a clean white coat to answer the door to the doctor . . . and tell Hannah that she's to keep the kettle on the boil till he comes, for he'll likely want sterile water."

He went off with a look at me as if we shared some private joke and presently he was back again to collect the breakfast tray for Hannah. His eyes came seeking mine, before he spoke and I knew he had made the excuse of coming up again, just to strike a spark off O'Brien for my amusement and his own.

"Hannah said to ask you if she's to send up the sterile water in one of the copper water cans, or is she to put it in the china jug with the blue stripe?"

"Jesus, Mary and Joseph!" ejaculated O'Brien. "The ignorance of lay people! Do you not know that sterile water is not to . . . ? Oh, well, never mind! I'll see to it myself."

She flounced out of the room with a rustle of starch and Gregory stood there still smiling at me. I thought it might be an opportune moment to find out if Dr Barry possessed the necessary attributes as a husband for O'Brien, and I asked him if he knew the doctor. I think he thought I was a little apprehensive of the impending visit, for his manner was reassuring.

"Very well indeed. Don't be put off by his manner. He was a surgeon lieutenant in the war . . . in the R.N.V.R. He's a dependable man in action."

He lifted a brow at me deprecatingly and added that he did not know if that would be such an advantage in times of peace, but he thought it would. Then he realised that he was not sticking to his character part of farm steward and might have given me some idea that he was himself a person of importance in the Navy. He picked up the silver box and offered me a cigarette, as he tried to cut himself down to the size of an agent to a broken-down estate again.

"Is he married?" I asked him and shook my head at the cigarette box, for O'Brien would kill me if I got ash all over the clean sheets.

"No, he's not married," he told me and he was relieved that I was off the subject of war careers, but I took him off balance with a sharp thrust.

"What did you do in the war, Gregory? You'd have been in the Royal Naval

Reserve, coming from the Merchant Navy, wouldn't you?"

There was a small interval of such silence that I could hear the murmuring of the sea off down at the point. All his old awkwardness was back in a moment. I was on a strange mental level with him and I knew that he meant to lie to me at first and then could not bring himself to do it.

"Yes, that's where the Merchant Navy went," he said slowly, almost painfully, I thought.

"An officer?" I pursued and he got vaguer than ever and shook his head slightly.

"I saw to signals and that type of thing . . . "

I had probed enough for one day and I had made him uneasy and I was sorry for it. I sat up in bed and hugged my knees with my arms.

"Well then, you're the very man I'm looking for," I laughed. "You can send a signal to Hannah not to let 'the Colonel's stove' run out of anthracite this morning, or the Surgeon Lieutenant will have no hot water to wash his hands, far less sterile water in the china jug with the stripe."

He picked up the tray and I knew he thanked me in his strange silent way for not persisting with the subject.

"I'll attend to it at once," he said and took himself off and I lay there and waited for the doctor's visit and was no nearer the solution of the mystery than before.

At lunch-time, when Dr Barry had still not arrived, I insisted on getting up and coming downstairs in a house-coat. I fidgeted about the sitting-room all the afternoon and to pass the time, I decided to explore Dermot's desk. It was something I had just not got round to doing, but I had no excuse to put it off any longer, so I opened down the flap to make a table and found that the solicitor had sorted out the chaos as best he could. There was one great sheaf of unpaid bills and another of correspondence. I sifted through them quickly and read letters requesting settlement by return of post, letters threatening to put matters into the county court. There were several notes from the manager of the National Bank, who it seemed had been a personal friend of Dermot's. One of them gave me food for thought . . .

'As I told you the other day, I can only think of one way out of the whole situation. Insure your life and step off the point. We'd get the estate on a working basis like that, but you'd not be there to take advantage of the situation, so that method is out . . . '

All these accounts would have been settled by Gareth's estate. I got a sinking feeling in my stomach at the thought of the spending I had been doing, since my arrival. The thought of any financial matter gave me the same queasy sensation and I had no confidence in my own powers of management. I decided to write to Mr Hood, my solicitor, there and then, and give him a full account of what I had been doing and to ask him to tell me how things stood, for there was still an enormous amount to be done. When I had finished the letter I put it on the hall stand to be posted, for Gregory always went into Ballyboy with any mail and he drove Gareth's car. I had sent back the hired car and had Gareth's shipped over from London and I had grown accustomed to the sight of it parked on the gravel sweep in front of the house.

I came back to the desk at last and went through the pull-out drawers, knowing that it was a task I should have tackled weeks before. In the right-hand one, there were all sorts of odds and ends . . . pieces of sealing wax, a fancy box of matches, an old fountain pen without a cap, some pencils without points, a pair of pince-nez glasses with a ribbon attached to one side. At the very bottom of the drawer were some photographs, all of people whom I did not know, except one. It was a photograph of Gregory, a younger Gregory, wearing flannels and an open-necked shirt with a cravat. He was standing by the rails of a ship with a pipe in his hand and beside him was a girl in a Wren's officer's uniform. She was dark and rather beautiful. I wondered if this was Dermot's lady. I did not think she resembled me much. I certainly had no claim to such loveliness. She was dark and her nose was a bit like mine, but that was all. She was smiling and she looked very happy and carefree. If she were Dermot's lady, she certainly had no inkling of the unhappy future that lay ahead. I put the photograph into the pocket of my house-coat and as I did so, I saw that there was writing on the back of it, in pencil so faint that I had almost missed it.

NELSON HIMSELF.

That was all it said.

In the other drawer, I found a gold wrist watch with a monogram on the back of it.

D.O'C.K.

There was a pair of gold cuff-links too with the same monogram. Then I found Dermot's ring, or so I thought till I picked it up and looked at the crest. I had been wrong. This was not like Gareth's ring, that I was wearing on the ring finger of my left hand. It had a wolf for a crest, his front paws held up in a boxing position, his tail curling behind his back. I knew it was what was called a demi-wolf in heraldic jargon.

There was a small spot on the inside of the ring and I scraped at it gently with a paper-knife. Some stuff like rust flaked off and lay on the blotting paper. There was more of it on the watch, when I looked more closely and it could only be dried blood. I sat there with my heart pounding up into my throat and knew that these things had been found on Dermot's body. Why had he not been wearing the ring with the phoenix crest that last night of all? Why had Gregory told me he had been wearing it? Perhaps there was a reasonable explanation. It might have been Felicity's ring. It might have been on the finger of the mysterious fisherman, who had come round the corner of the house and startled the wits out of Mary Bridget, but why had Gregory told me that Dermot had been wearing the phoenix ring? Was Gregory the mysterious fisherman? Surely not.

I put the strange ring on my finger and left Gareth's in the desk drawer. Then I went off to the kitchen for I had promised John-Joe that I would show him how to make crêpe suzettes, and I was not going to waste the rest of the day no matter what O'Brien thought.

I rehearsed him with the omelette pan for five minutes and at the end of that time, he was far better than I was, so I busied myself in making the sauce, while he got on with the production of a pile of delicious pancakes. O'Brien kept coming in with a crackling of her starched apron and she was quite put out to see me getting hotter and more flushed as the afternoon wore on. She was furious with Dr Barry for she had given up all hope of a professional call and had decided that he had not received her message.

"That strap of a girl of his had a man in the kitchen. That's who I heard saying 'Who the blazes is that?' She had no time to attend to her proper work, the way her head is full of men. It would have been a nice state of affairs if I had been an acute appendix, wouldn't it? I'd have ruptured by now. Think of that! I'd have ruptured . . . "

At last she decided that she would join in the cooking. She was a dab hand at frying pancakes, she told us, but she was of the opinion that John-Joe's pan was too small. She fetched out the biggest pan we had and put it over the electric plate and she fried a beautiful, thick pancake, ten inches across, using far too much of our mixture. None of us could find the courage to complain. Besides, we could always make some more of it and she was getting into a better humour.

"It's as easy as falling off a log to toss a pancake," she declared. "You've got to have the courage of your convictions. That's all there is to it. If you think you can't do it, then you won't do it! Let fly with the pancake and give it a little flip to spin it over . . . and it'll be game ball."

Gregory had come in as she spoke, but he stood quietly by the door, like a person might do at a golf tee, so as not to disturb her concentration. She tossed the pancake six feet into the air and it spun gracefully over . . . came down right side up too and she had the pan all ready to receive it. It was wonderful. She stepped back one pace and stumbled over a basket of earthy carrots, that Mary Bridget had laid carelessly on the floor. The carrots were catapulted out of the basket and O'Brien sat with precision right in the centre of them. A second later and the pancake had landed into her lap on the front of her immaculate apron. Gregory stepped forward to help her to her feet and there was a guileless look in his eye, that I suspected at once.

"There's a man coming up the drive to the front door, O'Brien. I think it might be that chap who was trying to sell us apples yesterday. I couldn't get rid of him . . . "

"I'll get rid of him," declared O'Brien, her face scarlet with the frustrations of the day . . .

She went through the door like a whirlwind and Gregory began to tidy the carrots back into the basket, remarking to himself drily that "that would put it in Brendan Barry's lap".

"It's not Dr Barry," I said in a horrified voice and followed O'Brien out through the door like a scalded cat, but I was far too late to stop her. She must have run up the hall, for I heard her fire her opening salvo.

"If you're the joker who's selling apples, you can go and peddle them in another street. We've had enough tinkers round

Cool-na-Grena in the last few weeks to last us a lifetime. Do ye all think this is a charitable institution? What's more, if ye must come here, we'd be obliged if ye'd use the back door and not come marching up to the front door as bold as brass, like the aristocracy and gentry."

"I don't think you understand . . . " said a man's voice, but she cut in upon him.

"I understand only too well. Do you take me for a fool? You're one of the boy-os, who don't know what it is to do an honest day's work. All you're good for is to keep your wife supplied with a baby every year . . . and send her out with the child in her arms, begging for decent people's charity . . . just to keep you in drinking money. I know your sort. Off with you now, before I give you a boot up the backside, that'll wipe that look of innocent surprise off your face."

"I understand Mrs O'Connell Kingston is expecting a child. I've come on a professional visit. My name is Barry. Somebody rang up yesterday . . . "

I withdrew quietly into the kitchen and found my staff uproarious with laughter.

"God above!" cried John-Joe. "Nurse O'Brien will murder Mr Gregory if we let her get her hands on the hatchet."

"It won't be as easy as falling off a log for her to get out of that situation," Gregory remarked, and I sat down on a chair and laughed till my face ached. I tried to compose myself before she came back and I think I managed it. After what seemed a dreadfully long time, she marched in with a complexion like a beetroot.

"May the divil fly away with the whole pack of you . . . " she started off and then she sat down at the kitchen table and laughed as heartily as any of us. Gregory went off at last to see if the doctor would take a glass of sherry and O'Brien raced away upstairs to get into a clean uniform. I was half-way up the stairs myself, when I remembered the fact that Gregory knew the Surgeon-Lieutenant. Shamelessly and with no possible excuse for such despicable conduct, I retraced my footsteps into the hall and applied my ear to the panel of the sitting room door.

"You're still as much a practical joker as ever . . . "

It was Dr Barry's voice.

"I thought this infernal business here might have taught you a lesson, though God knows it's no joke. Look at the position you've landed yourself into with your impersonations and what the hell have you been doing to that poor girl . . . throwing the dinner at her, by the look of it?"

"She was showing us how to toss pancakes, Barry. I hadn't hand, act nor part in it."

"Is it true what they're saying in Ballyboy then, that you've fallen for a girl at last? They have it that that's the reason you won't quit Cool-na-Grena."

"Perhaps . . . I don't know . . . " Gregory replied, but his voice was so low that I had a job to hear what he said. There was no difficulty in hearing Brendan Barry's words.

"Well, she's some lass, but she's got a blazing awful temper. But to think that the ladies have caught up with you after all these years, you that never looked the side of the road that a woman was on . . . and all of them dying from just one glance from the famous . . . "

I could have cheerfully killed John-Joe, for he came out of the kitchen door at that moment and I had to spring away from my listening post and pretend to be absorbed in the letters on the hall table. I took myself off up the stairs with what dignity I could muster and O'Brien saw me undressed and into bed. She insisted that I brush my hair and powder my face, though I pointed out to her that I was no film star. Finally she issued a tall order.

"Act as if nothing had happened. That's the best way out of an awkward situation."

I got an almost uncontrollable desire to laugh, but instead I thought back over the conversation I had overheard downstairs and could make very little sense out of it. Then John-Joe announced Dr Barry in a very proper manner and I was shaking hands with a pleasant young man and wondering at O'Brien's aplomb, as she moved forward with a rustle of starch.

"Good evening, Doctor," she said, her hands clasped demurely at waist level. "This is Mrs Kingston and I'm Nurse O'Brien."

It was as formal as any staged scene, and then I realised that O'Brien really was upset about what had happened and thought that it mattered. She had championed me often enough and the time had come for me to give her a little backing. I smiled at Dr Barry and gave him a horrible imitation of the Irish brogue.

"'Who the blazes is that at this hour of the day, Bridie?'" I said and he looked at me as if I had gone off my head. Then he sat down rather suddenly on the chair by my bed.

"God above, Mrs Kingston! You never heard that and I supposed to be out saving life."

Of course, that broke the ice at once and we were all good friends. After a while, he made a routine examination. He was very interested in the charts O'Brien had kept of my progress and he read them with his head very close to hers. If she moved away from him, he recalled her to his side with some professional query, in what I thought was a shameless way. It was obvious that he was very taken with her. He raised his siege upon her at last and came to sit on the edge of my bed, to tell me that everything was satisfactory. He thought our estimated date would be more or less correct and asked what arrangements I had made for the confinement. I explained about Dr Price and the Wimpole and he seemed disappointed. He tapped his finger against my tummy with a frown.

"So you're going to make a Sassenach out of the heir to Cool-na-Grena? Still I suppose you're English yourself."

"I'm Scots and Gareth was Irish. The child will have pure Gaelic blood."

He looked down at me intently and asked me why I would not stay in Ireland and have the baby in the country it belonged to and O'Brien muttered "That'd be the end!" and he was on to her like a shot, all his flirtatious manner gone in a flash.

"And what do you mean by that remark, Sister O'Brien?"

"This is a first baby," poor O'Brien said defensively, her cheeks pink. "It's an important baby too, not that all babies aren't important, for they are. Still, this one is all that's left to . . . Oh, well, never mind that now. This case must have everything that medical science can provide, to make sure there's no hitch. The child's not going to be born out here in the back of beyond, with no facilities in case of emergency."

He regarded her as if she was the lowest form of nursing life. Then he got to his feet and scowled at her very blackly.

"Dozens of women have their babies in this part of the country. Childbirth is a natural procedure. I challenge your fine record of morbidity in the Wimpole with my record here, in any cottage or house for ten miles in any direction."

O'Brien had no intention of fighting with him before me. She was a good nurse and she knew that the patient must never be upset of staff bickerings. I saw by the look in her eye that she intended to get him on his own and settle his hash for him.

"Would you like to wash your hands?" she invited him and opened the door to the bathroom, and he had, perforce to go into the other room. She followed him with a wink back over her shoulder at me and the door closed with an ominous quietness.

I lay in bed and listened to raised voices and what I presumed were hard words. I stuck it out for about five minutes and then I rang the bell for John-Joe and asked him to send Gregory up to me. When he arrived I explained what had happened.

"She's taken him in there," I finished, waving my hand at the closed door. "I think it's highly likely that they're murdering each other, and I wanted particularly to ask him to stay and have supper with us."

There was far more amusement in his eyes than the situation warranted. He told me not to put myself out and he tapped on the bathroom door and opened it.

"Mrs Kingston's compliments, Surg. Lieut. Barry. She would be pleased if you'd stay for supper."

"And would Nurse O'Brien be pleased?" came the laughing voice of the doctor, for he had obviously turned the battle into a flirtation by what must have been a most skilful manoeuvre.

"Maybe she will and maybe she won't," retorted O'Brien, and I could imagine the way she tossed her head, with the starched cap perched upon it like a white bird. "It's not much interest the doctor has in her poor opinion anyway."

"That's where you're wrong," he corrected her sadly, as if his heart was breaking.

He came back into the room then, picked up the chair and turned it round, sat himself down astride it, with his arms across the back and his chin down on them.

"Surg. Lieut. Barry has great pleasure in accepting the kind invitation to sup with Mrs Lalage Kingston this evening," he said with a twinkle in his eye. "Perhaps we'll be able to come to some arrangement about the price of the apples?"

"Get along out of that!" ordered O'Brien. "Let my patient get her clothes on . . ."

They went off downstairs together and I dressed and followed them later. I could hear O'Brien laughing in the sitting room as I came down into the hall and I thought that Brendan Barry would be the very man to marry her off to. My father always said that there was never a happy marriage, where the woman wore 'the trews' and I imagined that she would have little chance of doing that, married to Brendan.

At dinner that evening, the room was quiet and gracious. The brass lamp over the table had a crimson shade and pulled down, so that the corners were in gloom. The table was a rich red-brown pool of mahogany. We were using the crimson mats to match the shade and the colour reflected again in the holly berries among the Christmas roses. The silver gleamed softly. The whiskey in Brendan Barry's cut-glass goblet was a great topaz as he held it up to the light, and the claret jug was a ruby of immense richness. The carpet deadened all sound of footsteps and outside in the darkness, the night was cold and still. Far off a dog barked and then the silence took over again. We seemed to be caught up in an enchanted circle round the table. O'Brien was still wearing her uniform and her eyes were a vivid blue, that matched her dress.

She and Dr Barry were knocking sparks off each other. I was not paying much attention to what they were saying till I heard O'Brien challenge him with having some peculiar theories.

"I know human nature," he replied. "But the way the fashions change in medicine makes me lose all faith in it. It's as bad as ladies' fashions. Who can tell from one day to the next what length the skirts are going to be?"

"So you keep your eye on your wife's fashions too?" teased O'Brien.

"God above!" he exclaimed pretending to be horrified. "I haven't got a wife. What would I want with a wife?"

"I could tell you that too," replied the lady with a grin and he sighed deeply, his eyes flirting with hers across the table.

"I'm a misogonist."

"And what sort of religion is that at all?" demanded O'Brien, looking as if butter would not melt in her mouth. "Perhaps we'll see if we can't turn you."

I said very little. I sat there, watching them and remembering the days when Gareth and I had had just the same sort of nonsensical fun and I felt sadness that it was gone for ever. Then I looked at Gregory and he was smiling at me.

"Do you think it's safe to produce the pancakes, Mrs Kingston? Nurse O'Brien might insist on tossing them."

I wondered if he had sensed the passing cloud of my memory and was trying to dispel it for me. He was attuned to every nuance of my emotions and he was a gentle, kind person . . . kinder than Gareth had been sometimes. Gareth had been sparkling and vivacious and I had always been the quiet one. He had never realised the torment he caused me at parties, when he flirted with the prettiest girl in the room. I thrust back the disloyalty of my thoughts and watched John-Joe lighting the spirit lamp and putting the pan over the leaping blue flames. Dr Barry's hand was resting on the table by my side and I put my hand down on it with the demi-wolf crest for a fly cast over a trout pool.

"Ask Nurse O'Brien to toss a pancake, if you dare!" I said softly and saw his eyes go down to the ring. He looked at it in a startled way and then picked my hand up in his to look at it more closely.

"The demi-wolf, ducally gorged," he exclaimed. "My God! Would you look at that!"

He glanced over at Gregory with surprise written in his raised brows.

"I made a mistake then and you didn't put me right. It was the green-eyed lady . . ."

"Mrs Kingston must have found the ring in Dermot's desk," Gregory put in far too quickly, with a warning look at him, which he did not heed in the slightest.

"But that's not Dermot's ring," he said. "That's . . ."

Again Gregory cut in upon him urgently.

"He had it before the accident. Perhaps it belonged to his fiancée?"

There was amazement written in every line of Dr Barry's face now.

"That wasn't Felicity's, and well you know it too. Surely I can't be wrong about it? I thought . . ."

"It was in that desk in the sitting room," Gregory told him carelessly. "I expect Mrs Kingston found it there and put it on her finger this afternoon and forgot all about it."

"Of course, that's what happened," I agreed. "It was with Dermot's things. I intended to ask you about it, Gregory . . . "

I was telling a deliberate lie now, with not much excuse for it, but I had certainly caught a fine fish. It must be Gregory's ring and Brendan Barry had thought that he had given it to me, because I was the girl he had 'fallen for', the 'green-eyed lady' and not O'Brien as he had imagined. Maybe I could cast another fly over the pool.

"A demi-wolf, ducally gorged," I went on, almost to myself. "I wonder whose ring it was. It sounds as if it belongs to the days when knights jousted for their ladies' favours . . . all romance and honour and searching for the Holy Grail . . . "

I looked down at the soft rose gleam of the stone and then I sighed and met Brendan Barry's eyes squarely.

"Do you think it belonged to a parfait, gentil knight?" I asked him and saw him glance quickly at Gregory and away again.

"It belonged to a most brave and

valorous knight . . . " he began and for the second time in a few hours, I could cheerfully have killed John-Joe, for he chose that moment to tilt the pan and the flames caught the fumes from the sauce and sent a great flash of fire up towards the ceiling and they were all paying extravagant compliments to the chef and the subject of the ring was forgotten.

There was no doubt about it. Dr Barry was in whatever plot there was, up to the neck. If Dermot was still alive, Brendan Barry knew it. Did the ring belong to Gregory . . . the fisherman, who had startled Mary Bridget? Then why did he want to rebuild the fortunes of Cool-na-Grena? Dermot was the one for that. Yet there might be a third man, a relation of the family, who resembled Dermot and who might have a phoenix ring. Then O'Brien had seen the phoenix ring on Gregory's finger. It was a muddle. Out of the chaos of my mind, I shot a question at Dr Barry.

"Did Dermot wear a beard?"

"Indeed that he did, Mrs Kingston. I met him in the war and he had one of those Spanish beards along his chin . . . looked like a Spanish grandée. He got the job here for me, or I'd never have come to Ballyboy . . . "

Gregory might be Dermot without his beard, having substituted identities with the unknown fisherman. He would say he had amnesia and claim my child's inheritance. They would all concoct a story about not recognising the fraud . . . and even before Brendan Barry spoke, I knew that was all nonsense.

"He only wore it at sea . . . grew it to save shaving every day. We all did that. He was always clean-shaven at home."

7

The Heir To Cool-Na-Grena

CHRISTMAS came and went. I got through it tolerably well. Shortly afterwards, I received a letter from Mr Hood approving what we were doing to the estate. He urged me to try to make it as productive as I could and to cut any unnecessary extravagance. I had been thinking seriously of having my baby at home and this made me decide to do so. My decision was greeted on all sides with enthusiasm and at last I faced the ninth month of my pregnancy. I realised with surprise that I was beginning to be happy. Some miracle had started to resurrect my life from its ashes. I took it a day at a time and filled each day with business. I tried to work out just how my miracle was being worked. There had been work in plenty . . .

Far back in a secret recess of my mind, I knew that Gregory had filled some vacancy in my life. I felt some emotion towards him, but I dared not analyse it, in case it vanished like a mist. I admitted that if he went away, I should be desolate after him. After Christmas, I pushed all such self-analysis aside and turned the task force to the creation of a new barn to house cows and turkeys and geese and cockerels and I don't know what else. There had been a vast old structure there before and now we found that the concrete floor was sound and so was much of the timber. The galvanised had to be nailed into position, the doors found and rehung, the whole affair painted to a smart finish. It is impossible to describe what a difference it made to our ménage, for it stood in the wastelands, now ploughed to neatness. We put down cinder paths and brought up cobblestones from the beach for edging. We purchased day-old cockerels and turkey eggs to hatch. We ordered some young pigs. We even bought a cow. She was due to calve soon and the lady who owned her assured us that she was 'as easy to milk as a dog or a cat would be'.

O'Brien had been busy at the boat-house with the help of Brendan Barry. Brendan had taken to a daily call upon me, which O'Brien described as 'kissing the nurse for love of the child'. He was in love with her, though she did not seem to encourage him. Yet she would take no criticism of him from a third party and this I thought was a wholesome sign, for if I got her safely wed to him, I would never have to say goodbye to her . . .

The last weeks ran away slowly and then one afternoon, as we sat by the fire having tea, the first pains started. My physician was sitting on the floor at my feet, but there was no need to disturb the household. After supper, when the contractions were getting sharpened against the night, I whispered to O'Brien and saw the house organised like a maternity unit before my amazed eyes. Hannah bustled off to the kitchen to boil water, Mary Bridget ran home to tell her father, Brendan Barry went to the dispensary to fetch his kit. O'Brien mustered the furniture and fittings in my bedroom and bathroom into the semblance of an operating theatre.

By eleven o'clock, I was in bed trying to pretend that my arms did not belong to me nor my legs either . . . under the strict tutelage of my nurse . . . that I was going to sink down and down and down. Then after a time, there was a mask in my hand and I was taking deep breaths . . . and there was a miserable feeling engulfing me, that had nothing to do with the hurrying, strengthening pains. There was a loneliness of spirit, a hopelessness, a kind of panic, all mixed up together into a lost limbo of the mind.

"How much longer, O'Brien?"

Her hand stroked my hair back from my face and her eyes were warm and sympathetic over the line of her mask.

"Not long . . . not long . . . Hold on to the fact that each one is gone and won't come again . . . one less to bear. In a while, it will be finished and your child in your arms. Not much longer to wait now."

I turned my face away from her and a tear ran down my cheek to make a grey mark on the pillow and I asked myself why I should fear death, which would reunite me with Gareth.

My hand was in O'Brien's in a flash. Her eyes were crinkling at the sides into laughter.

"It's no good trying to be a heroine, Lalage. I told you to ask me when you wanted a spot of dope. You're determined to hold out to the bitter end, but you'll have your injection now. It won't harm the baby and it'll hurry things up."

There was a sharp jab in my arm and her cheerful voice advising me that there was no cause for worry. She had never lost a mother yet. Then Brendan was at her side and she was telling him that there was some sort of telepathy between him and her. She had just been going to send for him . . .

I am hazy about most of it. I was breathing anaesthetic with each pain, but sometimes I caught snippets of conversation, never intended for my ears.

"If he was the father, he couldn't be in more of a stew," said O'Brien.

"He'll be the father of her next. I'll lay you ten to one."

That was Brendan and he called O'Brien 'kitten'. I smiled to myself at that, for surely he must have felt her claws . . .

"She doesn't even know he exists. She's not over the other yet, but give her time . . . "

"This time next year, it'll be Mrs Gregory . . . We'll be man and wife ourselves then, Kitten!"

They meant that Gregory was in love with me. Another pain caught me before I had time to feel the surprise and O'Brien was beside me.

"You're not quick enough, honey. As soon as you feel the contraction coming on, take three great breaths. Don't wait to see if it's a pain or if it isn't . . . just fill your lungs with this stuff. You know how I showed you to do it."

The machine was snoring and it made a little click at the end of each breath, as if it turned itself off. I drifted down to some black land, where the pain could not follow me, though I knew it would like to have followed me. It stood outside and waited to see if I would come up again and when I did, it sprang at me like a tiger and I breathed great ungraceful gasping gulps and the sweat stood on my brow. Then I was back in the dark world again, though I knew that the beast was waiting at the gate again too. It seemed to go on for ever. I knew what it was like to be a mouse, caught fast by a cat, knew all the terror and the agony. Then a white gauzy mask was slipped over my face.

"Just take deep breaths now . . . deep, deep, deep . . . That's the way."

I fell sideways and out and away and I lay at the bottom of a deeper darker world, where pain could never come. I had only to stop breathing and I would die . . . only to stop breathing and it would all be over for ever and ever. Yet there was the baby to be thought of . . . and Cool-na-Grena. Cool-na-Grena . . . the corner in the sun . . . where there was happiness and enchantment . . . where the gorse smelt of apricots in the sunshine . . .

I started to rise up . . . and up a little . . . and up . . . up . . . up . . . There was a baby crying somewhere and I wondered why they let it cry on and on . . . why nobody went to it to see why it was crying. The darkness was greying at the edges . . . and the blackness was turning to grey and the greyness was vanishing like the mists before the dawn. Then there was a small click as if somebody had switched on a light somewhere and O'Brien's white gown dazzled my eyes. Her mask crinkled over her nose as she smiled at me and she had gone to see why the baby was crying, for she had picked it up and wrapped it in a blanket. She was holding it in her arms.

"Don't you want to see the heir to Cool-na-Grena, Lalage? Didn't I tell you it would be a son?"

Her eyes were like sapphires as she bent to lay the child in the crook of my arm. I looked down at him and he was Gareth, come back to earth again. He was as old as time in some strange way, yet he had all the newness and freshness and glory of creation too. I got a feeling of thankfulness that Gareth was not lost to me. Here was his immortality, just as he had said that day. Here was the proof that he had held me in his arms and loved me. I lay there and looked at my baby for a long time and then

O'Brien bent over me again and I put my hand up to the side of her face.

"You're the kindest person I've ever known, O'Brien. For the rest of my days, I'll thank you for what you've done for me . . . since the first day we met, when I walked into that room at the Home. I've been thinking what to give you, though there's no repaying the debt I owe you. Maybe you'd like the ostrich feather hat and the golden slippers . . . that never wear out . . . even if you didn't win the bet? You tried hard enough. If only I could get an apple from the garden of the Hesperides . . . it would be fitting. Do you know about the Hesperides . . . the nymphs, who guarded the golden apples? It was in a garden by the sea and they were guarded by a fearful dragon . . . just the way you've guarded me, O'Brien, so just as soon as I'm up and about again, I shall give you the golden apples of the Hesperides . . . "

"Well now, that's what I call a decent offer," she laughed. "Mind I don't hold you to it one of these days, but just for now, it's time you were waking up out of that anaesthetic and letting me make you pretty to receive your visitors."

"They'll all be in their beds and asleep."

"Of course, they're no such thing. They've been downstairs the livelong night and they'll have the tripes of their stomachs ruined from drinking tea . . . "

She set briskly about tidying me up and while she did it, she told me of the doings of the other inhabitants of my valley in the sun.

"Gregory has been pacing up and down all night, like as if he was on the bridge of a ship. I declare that he has a path worn in the sitting room carpet in a line from the fireplace to the door. Hannah is below in the kitchen and she's crying her eyes out, since the moment I told her that the new heir to Cool-na-Grena is safely landed. I can't get a word out of her but 'Glory be to God!' and what's more, she's started Mary Bridget Foley off crying too. John-Joe is scratching at the door there every ten minutes, asking if you wouldn't drink a glass of hot milk with an egg beaten up in it, for it would be as good to you as a glass of brown stout. The whole place is like a madhouse. The only one in it with any sense is old ‘Think-it-over’. He sat in the chimney corner all the night and no word out of his mouth, only his lips moving and his rosary beads in his hands. When he heard it was all over, he just stood up and he was as stiff as a stake from sitting in the one position all the night. ‘Yirrah! God is good!’ That’s all he said and away with him down the drive, as pleased as if he was a dog with two tails.”

After a while, I lay back in bed in my fresh nightdress, feeling sleepy and disoriented. Now was the moment, when Gareth would have been allowed in to visit me and to see his son. I wondered if it were possible that he had come through the door and was standing in spirit at my side and could see me, though I could not see him. I pictured to myself how he would look . . . how he would go out to the nursery, where O’Brien had taken the baby . . . how he would smile and say “Here is my immortality.”

The infant would grow through child-hood into adolescence . . . on into manhood. One day, he would turn his head and smile at me with Gareth's smile.

I slept for a little and woke to find myself alone in the room. I remembered I had had the baby, but I thought I was in London in my room at the Home. I watched the door for Gareth to come in, for surely they must have sent for him. I saw the handle begin to turn and the door open slowly and then in a flash, it all came back to me. It would be O'Brien, or Brendan, or Hannah. I was surprised to see it was Gregory. I closed my eyes wearily and knew that I would never see Gareth any more and Gregory's footsteps came softly across the room to my side. I knew it was no use lying with my eyes shut, looking back into the past, for the past was gone for ever. I looked up at Gregory and my mind was so hazy that he was all mixed up with Gareth, so that I hardly knew who stood there.

"Gareth . . . " I whispered.

He sat down on the edge of the bed and he put his hand over mine, but he said nothing.

"It was kind of you to come to see me," I whispered.

Still he said nothing . . . only looked down at his hand, which covered mine on the eiderdown.

"Do you like the baby, Gregory?"

He looked at me then and smiled, told me he had not seen the baby as yet.

"Hannah and the others are in the nursery, but I got the privilege of seeing you. I'm a sort of representative to offer our congratulations and say how pleased we all are."

"The baby . . . Garry . . . he's dark, like me . . . very dark not fair. He's very like Gareth all the same, only not fair. Gareth was fair . . . Gareth . . ."

I was drowsy again suddenly, feeling on the edge of sleep, as one does after an anaesthetic. The room was fading away all around me and his voice was fading in my ears, so that I could make no sense of what he said to me any more. I was asleep the next instant and I did not waken till the sun was shining in at the windows in the morning and O'Brien was standing at the foot of the bed with Garry in her arms.

"What in the name of God did you say

to Gregory last night, Lalage?" she fired off at me point blank. "He had a look in his eyes, when he came out of this room, as if his whole world was coming to an end."

8

The *Mary Cameron*

I WAS allowed downstairs ten days after Garry was born and a right royal welcome I received from the whole household. I found myself alone at last, comfortable in my chair before the sitting room fire. Then time put out a hand and turned the clock back for me.

I was remembering that first evening of all, when I had sat in the same place, disconsolately, rather like Mrs David Copperfield in the first chapter of the famous book. They had all come in to me, one after another, to offer me some help or comfort and now it happened over again, in a very strange way, that matched up well with the enchantment that was in the air of Cool-na-Grena. It began by Mary Bridget putting her head round the door and sidling in to speak to me, but she was a changed Mary Bridget from the girl who had stood wringing out her pink dishcloth hands. She had a fresh drill smock on and her shining pony tail was a model of neatness in its blue bow. She had discarded her Wellingtons out of respect for the sitting room carpet and she stood in her stockinged feet, but she was carrying a small pig under her arm . . . a black and white saddleback pig, from the recently arrived litter, brought over by Mr Slattery in his van.

"Isn't he gorgeous?" she whispered, holding him out for my inspection. "I knew you were dying to see my new family, so I waited till Nurse was busy in the kitchen and I slipped this fella out of the sty. He followed me all the way round to the front door, like as if I was his mother."

I scratched the pig's bristly back and he pressed his round hard snout against my hand and grunted his pleasure in being so formally introduced.

"Sure, it's grand to have pigs about the place again," Mary Bridget went on. "There's eleven like himself outside. You can walk down in a day or two and see them for yourself, but I knew you'd be dying to know what they were like."

She giggled suddenly in her irrepressible way.

"If they were to come in and catch me with a pig in the parlour, they'd murder me alive, but what the eye doesn't see, the heart doesn't grieve for."

I thanked her for risking her life in such a good cause and we were very merry about it too and then her face grew serious and she went off to the door and stood looking back at me.

"When I think of all you've done for me, Ma'am . . . let me work outside and got John-Joe for me . . . and the pigs . . . all the lovely things you've given us . . . and kindness always in your mouth and . . . Oh, God! Wasn't it the least I could do and you so set on seeing the bonhams, to bring one of them in here for you to talk to?"

She made her escape only just in time, for Hannah came in soon after she left and Hannah had the heir to Cool-na-Grena in her arms and was as starchy as Nurse O'Brien herself in her white coat. There was a new importance about the set of her shoulders and a warm content in her eyes, that had not been there before.

"It's a funny thing the way a family likeness will travel down the years from one generation to the next, Mrs Kingston," she said and sat down opposite me, looking down at Garry very lovingly.

I went and put the shawl back from his tiny perfect face and felt the tug at my heart again, as I always did every time I looked at him.

"He's so like Gareth, it's not to be believed," I murmured almost to myself.

"You're never done saying that," she smiled. "Yet you never knew Mr Gareth till he was a grown man, but I had Mr Dermot since the first day he was born . . . even before he went into his Mammy's bed. This little fellow here is the dead spit of him."

"You've never wanted to talk about him, Hannah. You know I hadn't met him and I'd like to have asked you about him, but you were so upset, I didn't like to. Perhaps you'd not mind talking about him now?"

She said nothing and there was no

sound in the room, only the ticking of the clock on the mantelpiece and the murmuring of the sea far away against the point. I thought she had forgotten all about me, forgotten all about the years that were gone, as if my baby had become Dermot O'Connell Kingston again, an infant in her arms. I went back to my chair and looked across at her.

"Was Dermot a good baby, Hannah?"

There was no doubt that Garry had taken away the pain she had felt at Dermot's death and she could talk about him again . . . could find some comfort in talking about him. My question had touched some inner release spring and the words came gently out of her mouth, while I sat there and listened to her.

"There was never a mite of trouble with him. I'd put him down after his ten o'clock feed and there'd be no sound out of him till seven the next morning. Like an alarm clock, he was. Then when he was bigger, he was never out of my sight . . . always trotting round at my heels, like a pet lamb. Good? He was as good as gold. When he went away to school, I nearly broke my heart after him. The old house was like a vault."

"He went to a boarding school?" I prompted her and there was loneliness in the sound of her voice now.

"It was beyond in England, a terrible distance away, with the sea rolling between us. Rugby was the name of it. I used to pack up his tuck box with cakes and jam, and off he'd go, trying to pretend he didn't care, and his face as white as a sheet. He used to write to me every Sunday. I've got every one of his letters still . . . all about how he was on the cricket team, or how he had scored a try at Rugby. That was why they called the game that . . . after the school, that had invented it . . . "

There were big gaps in the story, as she let her mind wander back over the years, pausing now and again, her face always soft with the love she bore for him.

"We used to keep a calendar . . . him and me. Every day, we'd scratch off a number. I'd write and say 'There's only five weeks and two days left till the holidays . . . ' Then he'd be coming home. I'd have the house full of all the things he liked . . . chicken for dinner the night he came . . . and chocolate cakes with walnuts on top. He'd get in on the evening train and they'd go to meet him at the station. I'd stand at the window there and watch for the car to turn the bend in the drive. I'd go out to the front door, to the top step and he'd come flying into my arms again, and the two of us not far from tears. God be with the days!"

I could see it through her eyes, hear the scrunch of the wheels on the gravel. It was so real for a moment that I would not have been surprised to see the door burst open and him come rushing into the room with his school scarf flying out behind him.

"Then he went away to the war?"

My voice shattered the silence like a flung stone into a still deep pool.

"He was in it as soon as it started. 'We can't let them fight our battle for us, Hannah,' he said, when I begged him not to go, but he wasn't at sea for a long time. That was a mercy. It was like the old days at school, though we hadn't our calendars to comfort us. He used to laugh about that, and his face as white as ever it had been, and he leaving Cool-na-Grena. He loved every stick and stone in the place . . . was never happy and he away from it. There's times I think he's still here."

It was a feeling I had experienced more than once myself and not in thinking that Gregory might be he, for there was a strange haunting of Cool-na-Grena by the memory of Dermot Kingston. I suppose it was only natural. I could sense him sometimes in the keening of the wind, that mourned outside my windows in the dark of the night and in the whispering sounds of the old house . . . the door that opened, with no hand on the handle, the curtain that moved, where no draught blew . . . the rustling of the dead leaves in the cool tunnel of the trees along the avenue, twisting down to the front gates . . . the silence, the dimness, the chill, that still lived near the stricken tree, where he had been killed.

"He met Miss Felicity at Chatham and a lovely girl she was, God rest her! She had eyes like the sea and a skin like milk, hair as black as his own. She was killed in an air raid. You know that. They were to have been wed the next week and he was bringing her home for the honeymoon. The pity of it!"

"They're together now," I said and I watched her face closely, but she only shook her head sorrowfully and after a little silence, she went on.

"He was near out of his mind, when he got the news. For months, he tried to follow her . . . did all sorts of brave things, not caring whether he'd be killed. Then he met up with an old friend of his . . . a man, he'd known at school. This man talked him out of his sorrow, for he had a kind way with him . . . told him that he'd see Miss Felicity again, sure as the sun comes up the sky. Then this man was moved to a different ship and he saved Mr Dermot's life. There was a kind of pattern to it all . . ."

"What happened?" I whispered.

"As far as I have it, there was a bit of France that the Germans had captured . . . a port, where the railway ran out to a pier. Mr Dermot was landed with a shore party to try to blow up the port. This other gentleman was in command of a ship that was to take them off, but it all went wrong on them. The Germans captured the French guns . . . sent in planes too, dozens of them. They pasted the ships that were lying waiting to take the men off. The head man of all thought it best to leave the shore party, rather than risk losing a ship. He sent out a signal to all the ships. 'RETURN TO BASE.' That's what it said. It was all in the papers. 'BREAK OFF OPERATIONS AND RETURN TO BASE.'"

"But the shore party?"

"The men had got out on the end of the pier, but the pier was blazing. They'd have been burnt to death, or drowned for sure, but this friend of Mr Dermot's . . . him I told you about, he was in command of one of the ships and he disobeyed orders. It was like Nelson again in the Battle of Trafalgar. They called him 'Nelson' after. Mr Dermot never called him anything else. He turned a blind eye to the signal and he sailed in close to the pier . . . shouted to the men to come aboard . . . and Mr Dermot was saved that day, God rest his soul!"

Her old face was full of pride and I knew who Gregory was at last. Dermot was dead and Gregory was 'Nelson himself'. Had I not seen his photograph? Hannah had given me my answer.

"Mr Dermot told me that it was like as if all hell was let loose out on that pier, with the planes swooping out of the sky like eagles, but they got them all off alive, every one of them, all naval men, the pick of the whole country, saved to fight another day."

"Or perhaps to come home safely to their wives and children . . . to come home to those that loved them, Hannah."

"That's a true word, Ma'am."

"So they made a great hero out of this man?" I asked her and she said that of course they had.

"But he said he was no more a hero than any member of his crew. He didn't like the fuss and the praise, for he was a quiet, shy sort of gentleman. He told Mr Dermot afterwards that if he had known there'd be such a pother, he'd have left him to fry. They were always laughing about it. He was a brave man . . . as brave as a lion."

I thought I had the complete picture

now. I kept my voice as casual as I could.

"And that was Gregory," I said and she nearly jumped out of her chair with the surprise I gave her.

"You knew it, Ma'am? God above! You knew all the time."

"Everybody knew it," I said carelessly, making nothing of it. "It was in all the papers."

She accepted this as sufficient explanation, though it fell completely short of it.

"They were as like as two peas in a pod," she told me. "Sometimes I get to thinking that Mr Dermot's come back to me. Do you know if you passed one of them in the house, you'd have to look again to see which one it was?"

"That's what John-Joe always says," I agreed and felt that there was no part of the mystery unsolved, but she shattered my complacency with her next words.

"Commander Frazer was a fine man," she declared and I wondered where he came into the situation.

"Indeed he was," I murmured, to pass

the ball back to her feet. "He was one of the finest."

"And so quiet too," she smiled. "But there's nothing he can't do . . . nothing. Look at the way he painted the outside of the house to have it nice for you . . . and the way he chipped out those steps in the pool below. He was at that job for two whole days and him like a drowned rat. It was killing work, but nothing was too hard, nor too much trouble to him, just so long as he was doing it for you."

My thoughts were racing round like rats in a cage now and I could think of nothing to say, so I held my peace and waited and after a time she went on.

"Look at the way he fixed up the old gate posts and got down on his hands and knees to dig the moss out of the front steps, but the boat was the best of all . . . fit for the Queen of England it was. LALAGE, he painted on it. LALAGE OF COOL-NA-GRENA . . . and love in every stroke of the brush!"

I was still confused. Gregory must be Commander Gregory. Why should Commander Frazer be at Cool-na-Grena and 'love in every stroke of the brush'?

"He told us how to say it too, for we didn't know. La-la-gee! It was like poetry, he said. God, Mrs Kingston! He worked from early morning to late at night on the old place and he kept us hard at it too. He'd start off as soon as it was light. I've heard him up at four in the morning. By night-time, he'd be dead on his feet."

"Commander Frazer," I put in tentatively and she solved another great section of my puzzle by her answer.

"Commander Gregory Frazer," she said. "It's a brave proud name."

"But why, Hannah? Why did he do it?"

She looked sideways at me for a moment and there was laughter in her eyes and cunning too and a great love for me.

"It's a kind of a secret between him and me. I don't know if it's fair to tell on him, but I've been thinking of it these last few days and I've come to the conclusion that 'tis high time you did know about it. Don't let on I told you, though, for he'd kill me if he knew."

"I won't breathe a word, Hannah," I promised.

"He knew Mr Gareth was dead," she said in a low confidential sort of voice and I asked her what that had to do with it and I was more puzzled than ever now, as she sat looking at me like a conspirator.

"He saw a photograph of yourself and Mr Gareth . . . one Mr Dermot had. It came over from London soon after you were wed. Sure, hadn't we your wedding photograph too, but it was this other one he liked. Mr Dermot showed it to him the night he arrived for the first time in Cool-na-Grena . . . the night of the accident."

"Photograph?" I muttered to myself, knitting my brows in concentration as I tried to make some sense out of what she was telling me.

"You were in shorts, Ma'am, and a tennis racquet in your hand. You had little white socks on and a blouse with no sleeves . . . and Mr Gareth with his arm round your shoulders and you both laughing fit to kill yourselves."

"I remember it now. We were playing

tennis with the McLeods. It was in Argyll. Gareth said I'd been cheating and he'd not put up with a cheating wife. It was all very silly . . . "

"Commander Frazer knew what you looked like, before ever you set foot in Cool-na-Grena. He nearly killed himself trying to get the old house presentable for you to come home to. He didn't want you to go away from it . . . didn't want you to go away from it or from himself."

"But why, Hannah? Why?"

"Because he was in love with you."

I jumped to my feet with the shock she gave me and stood looking down at her, shaking my head.

"Well, now I know this is all nonsense. Of course he wasn't in love with me. He'd never even seen me or spoken to me."

"But he fell in love with that girl in the photograph. God works in a mysterious way his wonders to perform . . . and when Commander Frazer saw you, he was more in love with you than ever. With every day that's passed since you stood at the top of the waterfall, he's more and more bound in chains to you, for he's come to know the sweetness and the gentleness of your heart."

I turned my back on her and looked at my reflection in the glass over the mantelpiece and wondered what he had made of the woman who had arrived in Cool-na-Grena that day. I must have been a vastly different person from the girl in the photograph, with my eyes dark from sorrow. There had been no laughter about the woman who had stood watching him come up the slope of the fall.

"He couldn't have known I was expecting a child," I put my thoughts into words. "None of you knew that."

"He didn't mind it," she told me calmly. "I went into the kitchen and told him that night . . . told him you were set of having a son. I was crying with joy as I told him and do you know what he said?"

I looked at her moodily in the mirror and I made her no reply, but she only smiled at me still.

"He said 'That's good, Hannah. That will mend her broken heart.' He made us all swear that we wouldn't breathe a word of who he was or where he had come from. He was a land bailiff. That's what you were to think, and he'd tell you the truth himself, when the time was right for it."

"So the ring with the demi-wolf *was* his, then?"

"Indeed and it was his, and is his. He swopped rings with Mr Dermot just before the accident. They'd sworn an oath that they'd bring the house back to its old elegance and not wear their own rings again till they had done it . . . "

I swung slowly round to face her and I thanked her for giving me her confidence, told her it must still be a secret between her and me and then the clock at my back chimed six times and she gave my baby into my arms. I felt the same rush of love for him, as he nuzzled against my breast, and as I fed him, Hannah went away over to the window to look out on the darkening sea and there was silence between us for a long time. I was almost finished my task when she spoke at last, her back still turned to the room.

"I've been waiting for a chance to

thank you for all you've done for me, Mrs Kingston. I wonder if you'll ever know the change you've brought about for me . . . just the same as you've done it for every single person in this place."

"It's I, who should thank you, Hannah, and well you know it too."

"I was tired and old and done for, Ma'am . . . like the poor old house itself. There was nothing left for me but poverty and old age . . . and a bitter taste to it too. You gave me back every single thing I'd thought never to know again, so that I wouldn't change places with the Queen on her golden throne. You've put your son into my arms, and for that I'll be full of thanks to you till my dying day. Oh, God! How can I find the right words to put on my lips what I feel deep down in my heart for what you've done for us all?"

I stroked the soft dark silken hair of the baby at my breast and pretended not to notice that Hannah was weeping.

"Never forget that I was homeless, Hannah, and you took me in. You were waiting for me, each one of you . . . and each in your own way, you stretched out your arms to me in welcome. Somehow, between you, you found me the happiness that I had lost and never expected to find again. I am far more in your debt than ever you'll be in mine . . . and there's an end to it."

She turned round to face me across the room, her rosy apple cheeks glittering with tears and her hands shaking a little as she held them out to me.

"There'll never be an end to it . . . and there never should be. There's not one of us in the house that wouldn't die gladly for you and yours and that's no lie, with the kindness and the gentleness, that's in your heart . . . and with the way you lifted us all up out of despair and misery . . . "

I decided that the conversation had gone on long enough and I knew by this how to bring it to a close. I knew too that if I spoke all night and all the next day, I could never convince her of the truth that the debt was mine to pay, and nobody else's. There was no virtue in protesting any more. Over the years and in my own way, I would repay what I owed to the best of my ability, but just for now, I held my son and heir up against my shoulder and patted his back and he smiled at her quite distinctly, though O'Brien would have mocked the three of us and told us that he was only bringing up wind.

"Did you see that, Hannah? He smiled at you."

She came over with her own face creasing into happiness, though the tears were still wet on it.

"Ah, God help him! And if he wouldn't smile at old Hannah, who would he smile at, the creature?"

Of course, when she had gone, it was Gregory's turn to appear next, in the pattern that was life at Cool-na-Grena. Hannah went off to put Garry to bed and in came Gregory to perch himself on the arm of the chair opposite me and look at me in his intent watchful way.

"I suppose I'd better give you an account of my stewardship. I was hoping that you'd have been able to walk down to the garden to see what we've done, since you've been upstairs, but O'Brien said it was out of the question . . . and of course, she knows best."

I protested that I would probably not be allowed out for the next year or two, with the care they were all taking of me and asked him to tell me what delights were in store for me, if ever I did get out to see the place again and we were very merry about O'Brien's harsh rule. Then he told me that the garden wall had now been restored to its original height and would withstand any tempest. In addition, he had not wanted to bother me with the details, while I was laid up, but he had bought three incubators in an auction in Ballyboy and Mary Bridget had them all at work, heated by paraffin and filled to capacity with settings of eggs . . . chickens, geese, turkeys, ducks. We had the nucleus of a successful poultry farm and he had no doubt that soon we should show a profit on the estate, that would satisfy Mr Hood. The cow had calved. Her name was Bessie and she was due to arrive from the farm in the next day or two. There was a section of the barn all ready and waiting for her.

He took out his pipe and smiled at me.

"They say that she's still 'as easy to

milk as a cat or a dog would be'. Mary Bridget is very excited about it and can hardly wait to see if that's right, though what experience she has had in milking cats or dogs, I can't tell you. There's no doubt, she's an expert ordinary milkmaid and she wants the skim for her bonhams. We told you they'd arrived . . . twelve of them. They follow her about like pet lambs. She takes them walking in the orchard . . . "

And further too, I thought to myself, but I kept the secret inviolable.

"So that brings me up to date with the news," I said and he got mighty awkward all at once and began to fidget with his empty pipe.

"Well not exactly. Molly O'Brien . . . she's handing the baby over to Hannah. She hasn't much excuse . . . but that's a long story. She's . . . she's . . . she's made me a very happy man, by something she's decided to do, but she insists that she tell you herself . . . and not I. You'll be glad about it. I know you didn't want to lose her . . . "

I wondered why on earth he was behaving so diffidently about telling me something about O'Brien. Then with a sinking of my heart, I realised that he was trying to tell me that she was going to marry him. There was no other possible explanation. Her flirtations with Brendan had meant nothing. It was Gregory she had loved all the time and I had been a fool not to see it. I saw that he had spent so much time visiting me in the last few days, only to be near me. Perhaps as Hannah had just told me, he had loved me once, but it was obvious that he had had a change of heart . . . and it was no wonder.

"One of these days, I'll have to weigh anchor . . . quite soon, in fact."

He would not meet my eye and he was getting more embarrassed with every second that passed.

"O'Brien?" I whispered and my heart was as heavy as lead in my breast, because I had to admit to myself at last that I was jealous of her and jealousy was a bitter, bitter pain.

"I mayn't get as good a chance to talk to you again. I'm bound to get caught up in the fuss of the wedding preparations. I wanted to thank you for keeping me on here, as long as you have, but now, I must look out for another berth. It wouldn't be right . . . I mean . . . I've been very happy here. I always hoped that somebody like you . . . hoped that. Oh, Lord! How does one put such things into words? If . . . if . . . if in the future perhaps, you want guidance or help . . . A son can be a handful for a woman to bring up on her own . . . and this place too. I won't be too far away, if you wanted help, and Mollie O'Brien will be near you too. At least, we've kept her here. The offer to put your troubles on my shoulders still stands, but there was something else too . . . "

His words dried up slowly and there was silence for a while. Then the stem of his pipe snapped between his fingers and he frowned down at it very blackly, his face far too miserable for any prospective bridegroom's.

"Something else?" I prompted him.

"Just to thank you for everything," he muttered, but it was not what he intended to say. Then he got to his feet and said he must fetch another pipe and he went out of the room without another word . . . and still the pattern of life went on unrolling in front of me, for O'Brien walked in with her apron crackling starchily and the little American nurse's cap on the back of her head. She thrust her hands deep into her pockets and stood in the centre of the room, just as she had done that first night and she looked me straight in the eye too.

"I'm getting married," she said and she was shy about it too, which was a strange emotion for O'Brien to experience.

"That's wonderful!" I exclaimed and tried to feel glad about it . . . and fell very short of being anything other than miserable, but she did not notice it.

"He told me," I went on. "Or at least he practically did, but he said you wanted to tell me yourself, and I'm so pleased for you."

"You never guessed it, did you?" she laughed. "With the way we're always fighting like Kilkenny cats. Half of the time, I ask myself if I'm only marrying him to be near Cool-na-Grena . . . and yourself."

"But he told me he was going away."

"We'll never go any farther away than Ballyboy. It's near your front gates I'll be to my dying day and I thank God for it."

I stretched out my arms to her and she came to kneel at my feet and I hugged her close and buried my face against her hair, so that her cap went flying like a bird across the room, and neither of us far from tears. At last she pulled herself together and sat back on her heels and grinned up at me. Then she retrieved the cap and perched it back on the top of her head, all askew to make me laugh.

"I'll teach that strap of a girl to answer the phone properly. That's one thing. '*Who the blazes is that at this hour of the day, Bridie?*' I'll give her 'Bridie'!"

"And what has she to do with it?" I asked her and she wrinkled her nose at me.

"We'll keep her on, of course. I won't have all that time for the house. I'm to help him with the practice . . . dispensaries and confinements and that. Mrs Brendan Barry . . . it sounds gorgeous, doesn't it? They say that doctors should marry nurses. Would that be why he's marrying me, do you think?"

I began to cry then in real earnest, but I was crying with joy, like Hannah . . . and wondering what on earth had got into me to make me behave so irrationally. At that, she got all professional and told me to stop being emotional, because too much emotion was bad for nursing mothers, and she looked so serious about it, that I began to laugh till I was quite exhausted.

"O'Brien!" I gasped. "I'm so happy I could die. Of course, Brendan isn't marrying you because you're a nurse. He's marrying you because you're . . . you're . . . you're . . . O'Brien, and he's a very lucky man."

"I don't know," she said and went back to stand in the middle of the room again. "We fight like tinkers, and he always gets his own way in the end. One night, I downfaced him and he laid me across his knee and spanked me as if I was six years old. That was the night I said I'd marry him, though I didn't say it for an hour or two after. Do you know, Lalage, he's the only man I ever met that

I couldn't get the better of, one way or another. Would that be a good thing?"

"An excellent thing, O'Brien," I said gravely.

"And when he kisses me, my legs are like two feather bolsters and my head is full of singing stars. Is that a good sign, do you think?"

I nodded my head and she gave a deep sigh.

"Ah, sure he wore down my resistance."

"I thought you were going to marry Gregory," I confessed at last and she jumped an inch with the surprise my words gave her. Then she came over and looked down at me closely.

"Are you gone off your head?" she demanded. "Gregory doesn't even know I exist . . . nor any other woman either. Are you blind, deaf and dumb, that you haven't noticed it? He's in love with yourself and with nobody else . . . hook, line and sinker, topsails, foresails, mizzen mast, poop deck, quarter deck, taffrail, ports, galley and hull. What's wrong with you at all, that you don't give him a word of encouragement? You know he'll go, when I go. He can't stay on here without putting you in a hell of a compromising situation, and he's eating his heart out for you. What's more, that boy of yours will need a father's hand behind him in another few years, and Gregory loves him, as if he was his own child, just because he's yours. You love Gregory too. Any fool could see that with half an eye. Why don't you tell him?"

"But I don't . . . " I started and remembered all at once how I had felt when I thought he was going to marry her.

She had walked off across the room and was standing looking out through the window.

"You're a deep, dark, silent sort of person, Lalage. I know there's times, when you laugh and joke, but there's other times, far more often, when you sit and dream. You get away on your own and we all know what you're thinking about . . . or imagine that we do. It's no use dreaming of what's over and done with . . . and it's sticking out a mile that you find him attractive. There's a look in your eye and a warm gentleness on your lips, when you talk to him. I'm telling you that he's breaking his heart for you. Why don't you say 'yes' to him and be done with it?"

"He hasn't asked me," I said simply and she spun on her heel at that and surveyed me narrowly.

"He must have asked you. He told me himself the other day that you wouldn't have him at any price . . . "

Her face was doubtful for a moment.

"Perhaps he meant that he thought you wouldn't have him. I don't know what ails him at all, for it's obvious that he worships you."

I told her she was talking nonsense and she ran out of the room, only to return in three minutes with his jacket in her hand. She tossed it into my lap and took a needle, threaded in black out of the front of her apron.

"There's a button off that," she told me with an expressive look. "Be an angel and sew it on for me. I had an awful job pulling it off without him knowing . . . and he inside of it."

She went off through the door and paused to deliver a parting shot.

"Don't go looking in his wallet. It's

not the done thing. It was Brendan told me what's in it."

I sewed the button on slowly and the thought of the wallet began to burn my mind with fire. I knew what Bluebeard's wife had felt, before she turned the key. My hands shook as I took out the wallet . . . found a photograph of a ship. It was a wreck, burnt out . . . hull intact, but the superstructure all blackened and useless. The name was clear across the bows . . . *Mary Cameron*.

There was a second photograph, the one of Gareth and myself . . .

I put them both back quickly and replaced the wallet in the pocket, put the jacket well away from me on a chair.

Then I sat by the fire and tried to work it out . . . with no success. There was a great chunk of my puzzle that I had in no way solved, nor was I to solve it for many months to come.

The time slid by very quickly too with the preparations for Brendan's marriage to O'Brien taking up most of our thoughts. It was due to take place in the autumn and we were turning Brendan's house inside out and upside down to get it ready for the new bride . . . and so the days slipped imperceptibly away while we papered and painted, and stitched and sewed, and dug and planted and cleaned and polished. Poor 'Bridie' took it all very well. She was a strong cheerful girl, rather after the pattern of Mary Bridget and instead of resenting O'Brien, she took to her at once and could not do too much to help her in any way she was able.

At Cool-na-Grena, our front beds were full of red geraniums and lobelia and sweet alyssum and the whole house seemed to have taken on the spit and polish of a battleship, every time we returned to it from the comparative confusion of Brendan's house. Brendan and O'Brien still carried merrily on with what seemed a love-hate relationship. She never once, that I saw, got the upper hand of him and she happier than I had ever seen her since the day I had met her, though she grumbled enough about "his masterful ways".

Still I had not solved the last of my mystery. There seemed to be a glass screen, that had come down between

Gregory and myself, that I could not shatter. I was shy with him now and he was more reserved than ever with me. I admitted at last to myself that I loved him, but there seemed no way of destroying this new invisible, intangible screen between us. Sometimes he spoke vaguely of going away, "moving on" he called it, and I felt despair again and desolation at the thought of being without him. At night, I lay in bed and thought of the burnt-out hull of the *Mary Cameron* and wondered if it was not the key to the whole situation.

It was O'Brien who put the solution to the mystery into my hand one Sunday morning in the autumn, as I sat on one of the white seats in front of the house and watched the gulls gliding down the air currents out at sea. She came running down the steps and put a copy of one of the papers into my hand.

"Take a look at that, honey, and burn it as soon as you've read it."

I took the paper from her and she stood there with her hands on her hips, looking down at me, her face very serious.

"Remember one thing, Lalage. If you

told him the moon was gold, he'd believe you. He'd get it down out of the sky for you too, if he thought you wanted it. You're a worse fool than I take you to be, if you don't put a stop to this whole ridiculous impasse, between yourself and him."

I saw the photograph of Gregory as soon as I opened the first page. It screamed out at me . . . WHAT BECOMES OF OUR HEROES?

There were other Servicemen, who had done gallant deeds, but I read about Commander Gregory Frazer, who had turned a blind eye to signals from base. It was all as Hannah had told me, but then I went on to what had come about after the war. With the sea murmuring in my ears, I found out the significance of the *Mary Cameron*.

He had left the R.N.V.R. and returned to the Merchant Navy, commanding a ship that traded between Glasgow and Buenos Aires . . .

After a while, I walked slowly along the short grass of the point, down the steps to the boat. The tide was at the full, breaking over the rocks of the pool, where he had carved out steps for my feet. I walked on round to the small harbour, struck flame from my lighter, held the paper like a torch, scattered the black ashes to the four winds. I thought how the *Mary Cameron* had struck a mine. I could see her in the darkness, ablaze from stem to stern, lighting the sea for miles around, with no ship at hand for succour. He had ordered the crew to abandon her and had stayed on alone. At last, he had left his dead ship. I imagined how his face must have looked, lit by the flames that licked the dark sky. He must have known the ashes of desolation . . .

The burnt-out hull had been salvaged by another company. She had floated for seven days. Then she had been towed into port. Captain Frazer had vanished after handing in his resignation, but the article could see no reason for it and neither could I . . .

"If Captain Frazer reads these words today in whatever berth he lies anchored, the signal is 'Carry on, Nelson. England is proud of you.'"

Why should he think it a disgrace, I

wondered. Was he mourning for *Mary Cameron* . . . in love with a lost ship as one might be in love with a woman . . .

That evening, at Garry's bedtime, events took another move forwards, for Gregory and I were caught red-handed by O'Brien, when we were feeding chocolate drops to the child. I had been warned before on the dangers of carbohydrate on tooth enamel, and indeed I was very proud of that first tooth, but . . .

Gregory and I stood there like two ratings, while O'Brien told us what she thought of us. I was a little worried that perhaps I had done something dreadful and perhaps it showed in my face, for Gregory took a quick look at me and then jutted his chin at O'Brien and was as arrogant as any master on the quarter deck of his ship.

"Hold your tongue, woman. You're upsetting Lalage about something that doesn't matter a tinker's damn. You'd think the child wasn't our own, with the way you carry on like a master at arms."

He swung on his heel and went off downstairs and he was no sooner gone, when O'Brien threw her arms round my neck and kissed me.

"Our own!" she cried. "Did you hear that? Why can't you knock down that brick wall he's built up between you?"

"Do you mean something to do with that ship?"

"For God's sake, you don't think he's after your money! Thinks you will feel he's after it . . . on the make. He's not a pauper. Of course, it's that blasted ship. He's under the delusion that he disgraced himself, by having that ship salvaged by another company . . . probably got a rocket for it too . . . You could make him see the light. He's a proud man and his pride's been dragged about. You could fix it and you don't do anything. I don't know what ails you, but if you don't do it soon, I'm finished with you . . . "

She glared at me with great ferocity. "I'll go off and marry Brendan and I'll never speak a word to you as long as I live . . . not even to say thanks for the lovely life you found for me. I'll turn in my grave too, every time I think of you for the next five hundred years . . . "

Her eyes grew luminous suddenly and

all the ferocity was gone.

"And I'll never wear the gold bracelet round my wrist, with its two golden slippers and its three golden apples and the golden heart, just because you said my heart was gold . . . which it's not. God above be my witness that I'll not put the ostrich feather hat on my head on my wedding day and it flown straight from Paris. I didn't even win the bet and look what you gave me. Look what you did for old Hanratty and he with a new cottage with a roof that doesn't leak and with a pension to the end of his days and work for his hands that he can do with pride in the work. Look how Hannah will be loved and cherished till the day she dies and she's laid in the grave. Look at the Foleys. They've only to wish for a thing and it's in their hands. Why have you slammed the door of happiness in just one person's face . . . and shut yourself out . . . and him too, from happiness? Don't you know there's no happiness for the rest of us if you're not happy too? Don't you know the store we put in you . . . the quiet one, who came to us a stranger and stole the hearts out of our breasts?"

Having delivered these harsh words in a disjointed way, she burst into tears and was gone, running out of the room and down the stairs.

9

The Flight Of The Phoenix

I HAD to get away from the house for a few hours. I could not bring myself to face Gregory again that evening. He might realise what he had said and be more awkward with me than ever. I suppose I should have followed O'Brien, but I knew she would only start talking of all the thanks they owed me, when they owed me nothing at all. It was little enough I had done for them, compared with what they had done for me, each one of them. I went downstairs and made some hurried excuse to Hannah, that I was taking the car over to a neighbouring farm to do some message or other. I would not be back till late, I said, for I wanted to go for a drive afterwards. I sometimes went off by myself like this. It was what O'Brien had meant, when she said I went away to look into the past and dream. The others might think that was what I was doing now, but I felt I must get a little distance away from Cool-na-Grena, both mentally and physically, and try to see things in a clearer perspective.

"Don't sit up for me, Hannah. I've got the key."

"But your supper, Ma'am . . . "

"I'm not hungry. I'll have a glass of milk before I go to bed."

I drove along the main road a little way and then turned off down a grassy lane, that I knew would bring me out on a headland, down the coast from the house. From there, I could look back along the edge of the sea and see the hills that hid Cool-na-Grena, and the tip of the point, and the tiny island, that lay at the end of the reef at low tide, and the backdrop of the mountains behind it all. The top of the car was off and while I kept on driving, the heat had been bearable enough, but when I pulled out along the cliff, it was oppressive. I sat there, looking across at my small kingdom and as usual there seemed to be an enchantment over it. I got an uneasy feeling that perhaps I was like Ossian, son of Finn, who had left Tir-nan-Oge and never been able to return to it again. As the evening darkened, the air became more sultry than before, for there was no whisper of wind. The sky reflected the dull leaden grey of the ocean and indigo clouds were banking far out on the horizon. The sea had an oily, smooth, swollen appearance, as if it might presently come creeping like a grey slug, up the coves and over the rocks, on still to cover the hungry grass of the point and upwards to devour Cool-na-Grena . . . then inland to engulf all the little gentle hills, with their orange-yellow gorse, and the roadside cottages and farms, where the kindly people lived . . . and the towns and the cities and the land and the whole world, till everything was silent and only darkness moved upon the face of the waters, as it had done at the beginning of creation.

What I had found out that day and what O'Brien had said to me just now went over and over endlessly in my head. I admitted to myself that I had fallen in love with Gregory . . . admitted too that my love for him was a stronger emotion than any I had experienced in my whole life. I blamed myself for faithlessness. I had loved Gareth and I loved his memory still, but this new feeling had engulfed me, as presently the sea might engulf the land. It had swept over me and caught me up and whirled me away and I was powerless to resist it. They said he loved me too, but if he did, surely he must have told me? Surely the burnt-out hull of a ship could never stand between us, if his feelings for me equalled mine for him. He was sorry for me. That was probably a truer assessment of the whole affair. Hannah's account of how he had worked for my sake to keep me at his side seemed very unconvincing, when viewed in the clear light of reason. I went slowly over the story of all that had happened since my arrival in Ireland and knew well that there were a hundred other possible reasons why a man should choose to stay hidden in this remote place . . . and not one of them had anything to do with a desire to be near Lalage O'Connell Kingston.

I got out of the car and walked to the edge of the cliff to look down, past the ledges where the sea-gulls nested, to the black rocks below. There was a sullen angry look to the sea, that I did not like, and a silence over the whole scene. Even the gulls were silent and there was no whispering wash of water against the cliff. The whole expanse of ocean was empty right out to the straight line of the clouds, which was rising well up the sky by now. I looked over at the point and it was lit by a pinkish glow from the dying day, and made it look like a stage set. It seemed a happy place, with no part in the gloom of the falling night. I shivered suddenly and went back to sit behind the wheel of the car.

What did O'Brien want me to do? Go to him and say "I love you. Do you love me?" Now that I knew I loved him, I tended to avoid him and be awkward with him. Never could I even hint to him how I felt. I knew it as the night came down around me and as the indigo clouds turned through purple to sable and covered the sky. I put my head down against my arms on the wheel and I stayed there for a long, long time and got no further with my problem. It was late when I switched on the engine and drove back along the lane to the main road. The night was stifling now and the elements had grown so threatening that the only bright point in the whole landscape was the winking of the lights of the headlamps against the gold lettering of the nameplate on the gates. It welcomed me home, as it always did and then the tunnel of trees swallowed me up till it released me again on the open space in front of the house. I put the car away and let myself quietly in at the front door. There was a light on in the sitting room and through the window I had seen Gregory sitting at the desk writing. He had stood up at the sound of my steps on the gravel and had turned towards the door to the hall, but I ran past it and up the stairs as silently and as swiftly as a mouse, for I could not find the courage to face him alone. It was late and the others would all be in their beds.

"Lalage."

I made no sign that I had heard him, but crept into my room and closed the door softly. Then without switching on the light, I made myself ready for bed, as stealthily as if I had been a thief in my own house, and knew that this new emotion of mine had driven out all logic from my head. I stood at the wide-open window at last and the night was silent and breathless, the sky heavy and overcast with the sable clouds. The light from the downstairs window still threw two oblongs of brightness out on the front drive and the brass of the sun dial glittered a little. Then suddenly a gust of wind blew in from the sea, with a strange warmth about it. It billowed the curtains out about me, but it brought no freshness to the sultry air and it died as quickly as it had been born and all was quietness again, till an owl screeched somewhere in the hills to my right. If I strained my ears, I could hear the tumbling of the waterfall, but the sound carried none of its customary coolness.

I climbed into bed and lay covered only with the sheet. I knew I would never be able to sleep and I forced myself to analyse my marriage to Gareth. It had been such a light, happy, laughing affair on the surface. Our friends always said we were well matched because he was so sparkling and I was so silent and deep. My love for him had been a pleasant thing, and it had been my pleasure to cause him pleasure. I had never seemed able to find the wild rhapsody that some wives claimed to have found, but it had not seemed to matter. I wondered uneasily if my relationship had been a superficial thing. This feeling I had for Gregory was as dark and as deep and as silent as the ocean . . . It was too hot to sleep. I knew I would lie awake for hours and that my mind would go round and round in circles. Then I was asleep, but it seemed only the next moment, that I woke to a clap of thunder right over the roof of the house. The curtains were blowing out into the room again and the rain was lashing the panes of the windows and spattering in upon the carpet. I jumped out of bed and slammed them shut. It was blowing a gale outside, the trees bending down before the force of the wind. The windows would be open all over the house, I thought, and switched on my light. It was well past two o'clock. I must have slept for hours. On the landing, I found O'Brien, her finger at her lips, at the nursery door.

"It's all right, Lalage. I've seen to the windows. The storm has wakened the child . . ."

We went into the nursery and she poured some orange juice into a beaker and settled a very sleepy Garry back in his cot.

"This wind is what Gregory would call gale force. God preserve anybody that's out on that sea tonight!"

Hannah had been disturbed too. She came creeping in like a ghost in her grey wrapper and bent to tuck the blankets more securely about the now-sleeping Garry for the night had turned cold with the rain. Then she made us some hot chocolate on the little stove she had. We drank it companionably together in the dim light of the shaded lamp and there was a feeling between us that night of comrades, who had been through battle together in the year that had gone and had emerged with victory. We none of us foresaw the grimness of the battle, soon to be joined. O'Brien grinned across at us.

"Doesn't it give you a grand feeling of safety, when you're in a fine strong house like this and you look out at the raging of the elements and think of the poor divils outside?"

"The fishing fleet was due out from Cloncashel last night," whispered Hannah. "God grant they stayed safe in the harbour . . . "

Garry had tumbled into sleep again and we went back to our beds. I lay there in the darkness and listened to the shrill keening of the wind about the tall chimneys. Now and again, the house seemed to shudder to its very foundations as a stronger gust whined in from the sea, but it had withstood a hundred such storms and would withstand a hundred more. I thought of the old nun in the convent in Limerick and how she had likened me to a little ant, that crawled on the pattern of life. I felt as tiny and as powerless now in time and space in the midst of the tempest. Before she had left me tonight, O'Brien had come into my room and tucked me up in bed.

"Forget all the hard things I said,

Lalage. It will sort itself out in the end. You've been happy these last few months, since Garry came. I've got a feeling that there's more happiness in store for you. Maybe, I'll get Brendan to drop a word in his ear."

"O'Brien, please don't tell Brendan. Promise me you won't. Please . . ."

She had gone off laughing and I lay and worried but not for long. The storm must have lulled me to sleep, and I must have slept for hours, but again it seemed that I was awake in an instant. The first light of dawning was coming in the sky and O'Brien was kneeling by my bed with her hand on my shoulder. The bedside lamp was on and the windows were greying squares in the darker shadows of the walls. I was astounded to see that O'Brien was fully dressed in slacks and a sweater and she was as wet as if she had tumbled into the sea. Her hair was plastered against her scalp and the water was running like tears down her face. She dashed her hand impatiently across her eyes and her voice was calm.

"Wake up, honey. Don't be scared, but

wake up as quick as you can and listen to me . . . ”

I sat bolt upright in bed with the fright she gave me.

“Garry . . . ” I gasped and she pressed my shoulder reassuringly.

“It’s nothing to do with Garry. He’s still fast asleep in his cot. Look, Lalage! There’s a ship aground on the point. I’ve been down there. Gregory saw the flares go up and he called me. It’s one of the fishing trawlers and she’s on the reef. There’s men aboard her. Get up and get dressed, honey. I’ve got your things ready.”

I scrambled into a pair of slacks and a thick oily wool sweater, that I used for sailing, shoved my feet into a pair of rope-soled shoes. She took me by both shoulders as I sat on the edge of the bed and she looked straight into my eyes.

“Now listen to me, Lalage. I’ve been down on the shore and Gregory’s there now. We’ve sent John-Joe for Brendan, but he’ll not get here in time. Gregory’s taken leave of his senses. I had to call you, because you’re the only one that can stop him throwing his life away. He’s going to take a line and swim out to the wreck, but if he does, he'll never come out of it alive. It's a woeful sea . . . "

I was out of the room and down the stairs like a hare. I took the last half flight to the hall in one leap, and her words urged me faster.

"He won't listen to reason. He doesn't care whether he lives or dies. You've got to stop him."

I tore open the front door and went out to the top of the steps and the wind caught me and hurled me sideways, so that I staggered and almost fell. The rain was lashing like a whip, with leaden shot in its thongs. The rush of the tempest tore the words out of our mouths and whirled them away to nothing. I ran as fast as I could to the top of the point and was frightened at the way the wind caught us, bringing us to a standstill sometimes. She gestured with a hand to the sea and I stopped up short for in the first grey light of the morning I could see the ship aground on the reef. She was half a mile off-shore, her timbers black against the white seething of the surf, that was breaking all about her. She lifted and sank back with each successive wave. It needed no expert sailor to tell that she could not last long, with the tearing of the rocks against her hull. I could see the crew clearly, drenched in the flying spray, clinging to any hold they could find, seeking shelter huddled together in the lee of the engine house, grasping at the rail. She was close inshore, but between her and the land, there were waves like a corral of white horses, that tossed their manes, as they rushed round and about, seeking to escape back to the freedom of the ocean.

There was no hope of any man of them coming off alive. For all the fact that they were not a half mile out, that half mile was a white hell of seething breakers and the coastline was jagged rock. I went down the steps to the pool and was appalled by the sight of the breaking waves, seen from sea level. They were coming in in rollers, thirty feet high, to break against the shore in a roaring boom, while the foam hissed and boiled. The spray rattled like hail against the rocks all around us and above everything was the shrieking of the tempest, with the wind veering now this way and now that. I shut my eyes against the flying sand and the flung pebbles, the stinging of the foam and the snarls of seaweed. Then I groped my way round the shoulder of the cliff and here I stopped short, for my legs refused to carry me any farther.

It was like the first day I had come to Cool-na-Grena, but it was a nightmare sequence of the first time I had seen them, Hannah and Mary Bridget . . . and Gregory. He had a line about his waist and he was shouting out instructions at the women. Old Hannah was holding the rope steady as she had done that day, playing it out to him round a bollard now and Mary Bridget was up to her knees in the sea, the waves breaking all about her, her drenched hair blowing around her face. I stood for perhaps ten seconds, as still as if I had been carved in stone. Then I had grabbed the wet front of Gregory's shirt in my two fists.

"Don't do it, Gregory. Please, don't do it. Don't try to swim out there, for it's not possible. You'll not come out of it. Nobody could live out there."

I went on babbling out words to him

with the wind whipping them out of my mouth. I do not know what I said, but I knew it was hopeless from the start . . . that he would never let the men drown out there, without an effort to save them. He took my shoulders between his hands and he smiled at me. I noticed how white his teeth were against the dark tan of his face and remembered that first day and how I had remarked on it then. He bent his head close to mine, his lips at my ear.

" . . . easier than it looks, Lalage. I'll go out on the lee side . . . drift back to the reef. I can do it. Don't try to stop me . . . no time left. She's breaking up . . . "

I looked past his shoulder at the black timbers of the trawler and prayed that she would go to pieces . . . prayed as earnestly as ever I had prayed in my life that she would be washed off the reef and go down, so that he would not have to go into that sea . . . and as I prayed, a great roller of green water, forty feet high, lifted her up in the air and she was gone, in a flurry of white foam.

"It's no good now. You can't go now . . ."

He still held my shoulders and there was a gentleness about him for all the wild fury about us, but his lips looked grim and sad.

"There's a ledge beyond that reef. She may be caught . . . out of sight. Who am I to believe a ship is lost, if I don't see it go down with my own eyes? If they're there . . . I'll get them off. Don't be frightened."

The wet stuff of his shirt pulled out of my fingers, as he tried to put me away from him, but I gripped him the tighter and screamed out to him in my terror.

"I know who you are. I know you're Captain Frazer. Don't go away from me. I can't bear to lose somebody I love . . . all over again. I love you. I love you . . . like I never loved anybody before. Doesn't it matter to you? You're throwing your life away. Don't you care what becomes of me?"

At that, he gathered me into his arms and held me so tightly that I could scarcely breathe. Then his mouth was cold and salty over mine and he kissed me with all his gentleness gone and I was a tempest myself, with the wonder and glory of it. My head was full of great coloured winds, that rushed through it and away and carried me up and up and up to a wild ecstasy, such as I had never known. He kissed me for a whole lifetime and then he let me go free again, so suddenly that I fell on my knees at his feet. Then he was gone, watching for a receding wave, jumping up and out and away into a great tall, curling wall of ice-green water. I knelt on the rock with my face in my hands for a moment and heard O'Brien's words in my ear.

"Pray for him. For God's sake, pray for him."

I struggled into the sea to stand with Mary Bridget and help her pay the line out to him and I prayed earnestly again and was ashamed and afraid to face God with a prayer because I had asked him to let the ship go down. I knew there would be little hope that He would listen to me now. As I clutched the rope and paid it out, inch by inch and foot by foot, I offered the Almighty all sorts of vain hostages in exchange for Gregory's life, least of all my own, for what would it be without him? I watched him fight the sea. He was making little progress, but still he swam on and he was a powerful swimmer. He would be carried aloft on a great rising mountain of water and then cast down into a deep valley. Sometimes, the sea rushed him towards the reef at great speed, but as often it dragged him back towards the shore . . . and little by little we paid the rope out or took it back again and every minute was a century in time. Then O'Brien was shouting in my ear again and I looked past her and saw Brendan come round the shoulder of the cliff with John-Joe at his side. He cupped his mouth in his hands.

"Go up to the house. We'll see to the cable . . . all available blankets and bandages . . . first aid kit . . . whiskey . . . brandy, anything . . . dry clothes. Hurry now . . . men on the back of the reef. He may get out there and get them off . . . saw them as I came along the top of the cliff. Hurry now . . . "

"I can't go away and leave him . . . "

I could feel the tears hot on my face, mixing with the sand and the spume and the spray, that was being flung in from the breakers. O'Brien had her arm about me and Brendan was taking the line from my fingers.

"Get along now. There's work to be done up there and the child is in the house by himself."

I gave a last despairing look out towards the reef and saw Gregory's dark head for an instant, before it disappeared in a flurry of foam. He was working up along the lee of the point, hoping to be dragged across to the reef and he was winning the battle foot by foot. As I watched, his head appeared again. Then a high solid wall of water crashed down upon him and he was gone again, but that was how it had been. We struggled up the steps in the cliff, with the wind threatening to tear us away and cast us down on the rocks below. Even at the top of the cliff, there was a constant hail of sand and pebbles and blown froth. We stumbled back up the slope to the house, O'Brien and I, sobbing with every breath we took. I had a stitch in my side, that was like the thrust of a dagger, but it was no crueler than the thought in my mind, that I had lost him for ever.

"God help him," I prayed silently. "Please, God, help him. Don't let him die."

Mary Bridget had prayed aloud down there at the edge of the sea, as we paid out the thin cable to him. With every foot of the line, had gone a gasped-out incoherent prayer to her saints to keep him from harm. Yet I had no faith in my heart . . . And now we had reached the front door at last and O'Brien threw it open. The wind rushed in with us and sent the letters on the table floating off along the floor. It was an effort to push the door closed again and then it was very quiet and calm suddenly out of the storm. We leaned back against the door, like two spent runners. Then O'Brien shook her head, as if she were a terrier coming out of the water and ran her hand through her soaking hair.

"Get every kettle or pot or pan you can find. Fill them with water and get them on the stove. Then bring all the whiskey and brandy and sherry into the kitchen . . . anything. Put on one of the electric convector heaters there too. Get the room very hot. Put every blanket in the house into the airing cupboard . . . off the beds . . . out of the blanket chest. If God is good, we'll have a dozen men like frozen, drowned rats on our hands in an hour or so . . . "

"And suppose there's no one?" I whispered and she took me by the shoulders and shook me like a child.

"None of that defeatist talk now! Don't think you'll not get Gregory Frazer back. After what you shouted out to him down there by the jetty, it will take more than an angry sea to keep him out of your arms . . . and in the meantime, you can best help him by getting things ready . . . "

I went round my tasks in a kind of frenzy at first. I spilt more water than I got into the pots and pans, but I settled down after a bit and soon there were gallons of water on the boil and the blankets all pulled off the beds and warming in the hot-air press. Then inevitably, we had finished what we had set out to do and changed hurriedly into dry clothes and I stationed myself by one of the front windows and the bad time began . . . the waiting in idleness. It seemed a hundred thousand years before three figures appeared on the cliff down by the point. The light was bright enough now to see that Gregory was not one of them. It was Mary Bridget with a fisherman on each side of her, her arms supporting them. Then at long intervals they came, always in pairs, some of them cut about badly from the barnacles on he rocks and still he did not come, nor did I expect him now . . . but I heard his name on every lip.

"The big wave took us over, but she stuck fast on the ledge. We knew ye'd think we were gone and the hope was dead in our hearts. Then he come clambering over the reef, laughing all over his face and askin' were we playin' hide and seek with him. We rigged a cable to the shore then in no time . . . and he was still laughing, with the wind tossing his laughter up against the sky . . .

"He's out on that reef still, and 'tis a woeful place. He'll not stir off it, till the last man's safe ashore. Old Pat was agen gettin' into the water, once he was out of it. He said he'd sooner stick to the rocks and have done, but your man out there picked him up like a babby and threw him down into my arms. 'Pat can't swim,' says he. 'Maybe you'll teach him on the way in to the shore . . . '

"If he's not off soon, 'twill be too late for him. The tide's running in fast and the water'll be over his head in the half hour. The cable keeps fraying agen the sharpness of the rock and it was slowing us up, for we had to unhitch it and make it fast agen and no time at all left to us . . .

"He sent us in two by two . . . 'like the animals in the ark,' says he, 'though Noah only had the rain to contend with, and not a raging sea as well.' You couldn't help laughing at the things he said, and he kep' our spirits raised with the way he didn't give a damn for the storm. 'There's nothing to it at all,' says he. 'I've been through that patch of water once, so I know what I'm talking about. Let a man that can swim team up with one that can't . . . and on the way in, don't forget that there's plenty of hot rum waiting for you above in

Cool-na-Grena.'"

We had turned the kitchen into a first-aid post and Brendan had come up from the shore and was working at the table, stitching up cuts, bandaging, splinting. O'Brien and he were working as a team and she had everything ready to his hand before he had time to ask for it. She looked as fine a nurse in her old slacks and sweater, with her wet hair still clinging to her head, as ever she had been in her starched trim uniform. The room seemed full to capacity, for we had men lying on the floor on mattresses and men on chairs with blankets round their shoulders, men struggling into the dry clothes we had found for them. I was working as hard as ever I had worked in my life and trying not to rush out to the front windows to watch the path from the point. There was a feeling of foreboding in my chest like packed ice, that his praises, sung on every side, did nothing to melt. I was desolate, because I knew I had left it too late to tell him I loved him. Yet there was such confusion and excitement and such coming and going, that time was slipping by. Soon there was an ambulance and later cars, to shuttle back and forth to Cloncashel, fifteen miles along the coast. The Coastguards were there and gone again and a Civic Guard from Ballyboy was trying to take statements and not succeeding in the least, and still the news dribbled in to us.

"There's a host of helpers below on the strand now, Ma'am, but himself is still on the reef with Patcheen Kelly with the seas washing over them . . . "

"The poor old *Rose of Sharon* will never put out from Cloncashel Harbour any more. She's coming in now. The water's afloat with her timbers. The binnacle lamp was flung down at my feet ten minutes ago, and I coming along the jetty . . .

"Had the sea been running the other way, we could have come in on the strand. The rocks is terrible hard work to land on, but if he'd tried it from the sand, he couldn't have come out to us. Shure, he knows the tides like he knows the palm of his hand."

Over in the corner of the kitchen, a half-grown man-boy knelt with his rosary beads in his hand, with no shame that he prayed aloud and I would have given much to have the courage to kneel at his side.

"... Holy Mary. Mother of God, pray for us sinners now and at the hour of our death ..."

I could not bear it any more. There was a lull in the activities, while we waited for the last men to come in. I slipped round the door and out to the sitting room, to gaze with aching eyes along the path. A group of Civic Guards were standing with one of the Coastguards a hundred yards away, but except for them, the path was empty. Then Brendan was at my elbow.

"Is it weary waiting for him to come, Lally?"

I pressed my hands together as if I prayed and perhaps I did pray, but I said nothing.

"He'll be the last off that reef. It was the same story on the *Mary Cameron* ... covered himself in glory then too, and himself blind to it, because he hadn't been right about the loss of the ship. You know that, don't you? You know what was wrong with him, that he hid up here like a wounded animal . . . chose to think he was disgraced, because the bloody company gave him a rocket. Blast their souls to hell! I'd like to see one member of the Board come out of it the way he did. All the sea they knew was the fortnight they spent in Frinton or Bognor, when they took their wives along for a breath of sea air and to show off their diamonds. God above! Show me a man who knows what the sea can do, that had a word of blame for your man out there on the reef now. You know the full story, don't you?"

I shook my head and watched the path still, as he gave me the last little section of my jig-saw.

"He was the skipper of the *Mary Cameron*. She struck a mine in mid-ocean and took fire . . . blazed from bow to stem in the pitch black of the night. He got the whole crew off alive . . . every last man of them and it was no easy task he had, for there was panic among the Lascars. The boats were all away by the time he decided to abandon ship himself. He'd even given his life-jacket to a bloody fool that'd lost his own, so he just went in off the side and swam away from the ship . . . didn't get far before the tanks went up. There was one hell of an explosion and he was knocked senseless. When he came to himself again, there was nothing but the darkness. Then he was picked up after a long time by one of the boats. He presumed that the ship had gone down, reported it that way, but she hadn't. The explosion had blown out the fire and she drifted around for a week before she was salvaged. A ship belonging to some other company towed her into port . . . "

"A burnt-out hull wouldn't have any value . . . " I whispered, and he told me I was wrong about that.

"A wreck like that is worth thousands of pounds for scrap, but she was fully covered for insurance. It was no skin off anybody's nose, but the company gave him a rocket . . . and the publicity! God above, they went to town on that. He was such a hero from the war days, that he was headline news. Everywhere he went, there were reporters and photographers . . . and he's a shy man.

He felt disgraced too . . . "

"He can't have felt disgraced. He'd done nothing wrong."

"You and I could never understand it, Lally, not in a hundred years. He'd left his ship, and she had still floated. She floated without a crew and I suppose he argued that he had deserted her in her hour of need. I know we could tell him that if he had stayed aboard, he'd have been killed in the explosion, but all he could feel was that he had deserted her . . . and a skipper loves his ship. Perhaps he fretted about the fact that the hull was a danger to other shipping. I don't know. I don't even understand, for I was only a war-time sailor and a doctor at that. Gregory Fletcher has the sea in his veins. Besides, he's an idealist and a dreamer . . . and he runs before the roar of the crowd."

I turned round to face him at last and told him what Gregory had said to me before he went into the sea.

"'Who am I to believe a ship is lost if I don't see it go down with my own eyes?' That's what he said. I couldn't stop him going, even though the trawler was gone out of our sight. I told him I loved him . . . but still he went."

He put his arm through mine then and led me out to the hall and he repeated what O'Brien had told me.

"If he knew that, he'll be back. It would take more than the Atlantic Ocean in a bad temper to keep him away from Cool-na-Grena, if he knows you love him. He thought you couldn't get Gareth out of your mind. He was breaking his heart over it. Today he's just doing something he thought he had to do . . . proving himself, though there was no need for Frazer to prove himself to any man . . . only to prove himself to himself, if you know what I mean. Thank God! He'll have done it by now."

He looked down at me and smiled.

"Get a hold of some of the blankets and make up his bed. All the beds in the house are torn to pieces and we'll want one ready. Get it made up nice and snug. Put two hot bottles in it . . ."

His eyes were mischievous suddenly and he took my chin in his hand.

"It would be far better if you climbed into it yourself and got it warmed up for him, while you're waiting, but I daresay that's out of the question, for you're a decent-living woman, or so Mollie O'Brien tells me."

I pulled away from him and he laughed at my embarrassment. Then his face was serious.

"One of the men told me they're hauling him on the line at any moment now. God willing, it'll be an easier trip to the shore than it was for him out to that reef. He'll just about make it, but he'll be spent after this morning's work. Get that bed ready as quick as you can."

I ran along to the kitchen and filled two hot-water bottles. Then I gathered up some blankets and went up the stairs to his room. It was a very monastic place, with one window looking out to the sea at the side of the house and one that had the whole panorama of the mountains behind for a back-drop. There was a bed, a chest of drawers with a mirror on top of it, a wardrobe. On the chest of drawers, his brushes were laid out neatly, silver-backed and crested with the demi-wolf, if I had but looked at them before. It seemed a thousand years since I had yanked all the blankets off the bed with my heart thumping against my ribs, in just the same way as it was thumping now, as I got out fresh sheets and made the bed up again. I filled a hot bath in the room next door, turned on the electric fire, set fresh pyjamas before it and his silk dressing gown. I stood and let the heavy fringed silk of the tassel run through my fingers, as I looked out at the mountains and watched the clouds scudding across them. The wind was dying down a little, though it still twisted the trees down before it. Through the side window, I could see the waterfall he had contrived for my pleasure and my breast ached at the sight of it now. Down at the jetty, the scene would be still the same. I remembered the flung pebbles and sand and spume . . . remembered the sea coming in in smooth great rollers to break into bubbling seething insanity. I had declared my love for him openly . . . never even given him time to speak for himself and tell me he loved me too. I was shy of him now and it was impossible for me to go out to one of the front windows and watch for him to come . . . impossible for me to go running down the stairs to meet him at the front door. I stood there, running the tassel of the dressing gown through my fingers . . . and I waited, so I missed what O'Brien spoke of ever afterwards as "the Return of the Conquering Hero".

He came striding in jauntily, she said, looking like an Indian chief, with a striped blanket draped round his shoulders, his wet head as black as a crow. He had a Coastguard flanking him at either side, a correct half pace to the rear . . . and he was not Gregory any more, but Captain Frazer. According to O'Brien he was all 'top-brass' and "Aye, aye, sir. Permission to speak, Captain, sir." She said that every man in the kitchen practically sprang to attention and saluted him, as he came through the door, and his eye went round the room looking for me, or so she had it. He dismissed the poor Civic Guard, who was still trying to take statements with as lordly an air as if he said "Get off my bridge, blast you!" and he was mighty sharp with any of the seamen or anybody else either, who attempted to thank him or to utter any word of praise for what he had done. He sorted them all out. . . packed the last of them into the cars and got them off the premises. Then he set the others to various tasks about the house . . . saw that everything was shipshape and Bristol fashion. She made quite a story out of it, O'Brien. He shooed the women out of the kitchen, all except O'Brien and she didn't count, or so she said, because she was a nurse. Then he changed into dry clothes and asked her where I was . . .

I have no reason to doubt her description for in the years to come, I was to know the masterly side to him too, but there was no 'top-brass' about him, and no masterliness either, when he came through the door of his bedroom, looking for me. He was very little different from the first day I had seen him, coming out on the top step of Cool-na-Grena to welcome me home. He was shy and a little diffident and his hair was blacker than ever with sea water. He was wearing the pair of faded khaki slacks and the white roll-topped sweater that we had had waiting for him before the kitchen fire.

I had turned towards him and he closed the door behind him and stood with his back to it, just looking at me, searching my face with his eyes and saying nothing for a long time. Then he held out his arms to me and I went across the room to him and was gathered fiercely against his chest. His voice spoke against the top of my head.

"It was a bit noisy down there. You did say those things . . . I thought you said . . . or did you? Perhaps you only said them to try to stop me? Afterwards I wondered . . . out there on the reef, I kept asking myself. You said you knew my name was Frazer. Then you said you loved me . . . not once, you said it, but many times . . . "

I could not speak to save my life. I just put my arms around him and held him as if I never wanted to let him go again . . . laid my face in against the coldness of his neck.

"Did you mean it?"

I nodded my head, but he held me away from him and searched for the truth in my eyes . . . and found it. Then his mouth came down over mine and the whole room tilted and spun around me and great stars seemed to swell and burst inside my head. I knew what it was at last to be burnt up like the phoenix, to stand in the glory of the leaping flames, completely reborn, completely restored, burnt up and consumed in a great holocaust of ecstasy . . . transported to the outer spaces of joy.

At last I put my hands to his face and felt the coldness of it, so I took myself out of his arms and told him that he was supposed to be soaking in a hot bath. He laughed at that and made great fun of the idea, but I put his pyjamas and dressing gown in his hands and pushed him out of the room . . . warned him that he was to stay in the bath for half an hour at least. He was back again within five minutes, in the blue pyjamas now, with the dressing gown draped round his shoulders and without further ado, I tucked him up in bed, while he grumbled at me that I was getting as bad as O'Brien . . . grumbled that he never slept with hot bottles in his bed, that it was a womanish trick . . . that he would not even stay in bed, if I did not sit on the edge of it and talk to him, and for mercy's sake to turn off the electric fire, for the room was too hot and he was not a hot-house plant, but if I was cold, to leave it on . . . yes, it was better left on . . . yes, of course he wanted it and it was not just for my sake.

"I must talk to you, Lalage. I've got so much to explain to you . . . "

I sat on the edge of the bed and held his hand in mine and told him I knew it already. If it was about the *Mary Cameron*, I told him, I knew all about that too, and he had been foolish to blame himself . . . He was very tired. He turned his head on the pillow to watch me and I thought it best to let him talk on . . . that he would talk himself to sleep like a child.

"The *Mary Cameron* . . . I wanted to forget all about her . . . hide away from the limelight. I was sick of it. I thought of Cool-na-Grena. I came here to Dermot . . . knew he'd not turn me away. He told me what you've just said . . . that I wasn't to blame for it. I couldn't see it like that. He was mourning for Felicity. I tried to persuade him to get the house on its feet again . . . by sheer hard work . . . drive out heartbreak. He couldn't do it alone, or so he said . . . asked me to help him . . . made me promise. There was all this business about the rings, that puzzled you. We changed rings . . . swore an oath . . . very childishly, I suppose, looking back on it now. That's how he came to be wearing mine. I thought I shouldn't take mine back till I'd fulfilled my side of the bargain. I was still there . . . and Dermot was dead . . ."

He closed his eyes and turned his head away from me and I wondered if he was reliving that July night.

"There was a thunderstorm. We stood at the window downstairs and watched the lightning over the sea. He told me he was sorry I had rescued him from the shore operation. If he'd been killed, the estate would have gone to Gareth. He brought down photographs of Gareth and you . . . said that Gareth was wealthy enough to get the house on its feet again, but he hadn't much faith that he'd do it. You were different . . . country born and a Scot. You'd make Gareth have mercy on the old house. It was like the one you'd been born in in Argyll. He thought, if you came over and saw it, you'd not see it die . . . "

His voice was very weary but his words went stumbling on.

"He thought it . . . wasn't sure. He'd never met you . . . knew nothing about you . . . wanted me to look at your photograph . . . see what I thought . . . "

He looked back at me now, his eyes dark.

"I fell in love with the girl in the photograph . . . if ever you heard of such a thing. She was the one I had waited for all my life, but she was married . . . and very much in love with her young husband . . . "

I put up a hand to stroke back the lock of hair that fell over his forehead and told him to go to sleep, that we would talk about it later, but still he went on.

"It stopped raining after supper and the moon came out. The squall had almost blown itself out. The air was cool and fresh . . . blowing in from the sea. We went down to the landing stage . . . lot of sea running. The boat was adrift . . . wood of the mooring post was rotten. It took us hours to get it secured. Then we climbed back up the cliff . . . looked at the house . . . wonderful in the moonlight. It had lost its uncared-for look. You couldn't see the chipping paint . . . nor the tattered state of the carpets and curtains . . . the worm-eaten furniture . . . the rottenness of the whole structure . . . the despair inside. I told Dermot it would look just like that in a few years, when we had rebuilt its fortunes . . ."

"It looks like that now," I whispered, but he hardly noticed that I had spoken, for he was lost in another world.

"We walked through the tunnel of trees . . . planned to go as far as the road, before we turned in for the night. You know how dense the trees are . . . shut out the light. We never noticed that the moon had gone in and that the storm was blowing up again. We came out of the trees . . . down by the gate. He turned to me . . . said a strange thing. Perhaps he saw into the future at that moment. 'You're the one who'll do it,' he said. 'You and the others . . . not me. I want to see Felicity again . . . '"

His face was screwed up in the bitterness of the memory and his voice was jerky and unhappy now, but I knew it was best to let him get it all told, so I made no move, beyond my stroking of his forehead still.

"There was a crack like a whip . . . don't remember much about it. I came to and found I'd been thrown into the undergrowth . . . couldn't see him. It was pitch black and the rain was pouring down. I tried to strike matches, but it was a fool's task . . . wet. After a bit, I got back to the house . . . knocked the women up. Hannah found a storm lantern and I went back by myself . . . no use letting them come with me . . . knew he was done for . . . pretty certainly . . . found him, after a long time . . . seemed a long time. The whole weight of the chestnut tree had caught him . . . the leaves were lying all around and his hand was out . . . stretched out with my ring on it. I left it like that . . . had to keep telling myself that he was with Felicity again. It wasn't Dermot any more. I was sorry that I had turned back and taken him off that pier . . . sorry . . . sorry. I had seen plenty of that sort of thing in action, but this was . . . my friend . . . Dermot . . . Men came at last . . . helped me . . . there was the funeral. I was in the house then, not knowing what to do. Then a wire came to say that Gareth was dead too . . . thought I could see the hand of God in it . . ."

I had slid down to my knees by the bed and I put my cheek against his to comfort him and he held me in his arms and put up a hand to stroke my hair.

"I thought what Gareth's death must be doing to you. They said you were ill . . . in a nursing home. Nobody mentioned the baby . . . not till you told us that night. I had sworn not to leave the place and I didn't want to then anyway . . . started to work on it. Then you wrote to say you were coming over. I tried to get it to look better . . . didn't want you to go away again. I made them promise to say I was the steward, but it was a foolish plan. I made a mess of it right from the start."

"You were fine," I said and rubbed my cheek against him like a cat, till he took my chin in his hand and looked at me.

"The first moment I saw you, I knew that everything I had thought about you was true . . . knew I'd love you till the day I died, but it was like Dermot . . . all over again. I saw your eyes, saw you push your nails into the palms of your hands . . . crucifying yourself on the cross of your sorrow. I could do nothing to help you . . . only hope that your life would be rebuilt like Cool-na-Grena. Perhaps that's what's happened. I don't know."

Perhaps he caught a fleeting sorrow in my eyes, for he let go my chin all at once and raised himself up on one elbow, all his sleepiness forgotten and his mouth as grim and sad, as it had been down at the wreck, when he had spoken about not believing a ship had been lost, unless he saw it with his own eyes.

"Even now, I can't believe you've come to love me. It's been such a long time . . . seemed so at any rate. I never hoped . . . never thought . . . God! If you knew how often I've tried to tell you, knowing it would be useless . . . and perhaps it still is useless. Did you say that today, down on the shore, just to stop me going into the sea?"

I put my hand on his shoulder and settled him back on his pillows again, held his face between my two hands then and looked into his eyes.

"Down on the shore this morning, I prayed that the trawler would wash off the reef and go down, so that you wouldn't have to risk your life. I'll be ashamed of that prayer till my last day on earth, but if it happened all over again, I'd act the same way all over again. I'd have seen every man on the *Rose of Sharon* dead, before I'd willingly have let you do what you did. I know it was sinful and selfish, but I couldn't help it. I'd seen everybody in the world gone . . . everything I possess lost . . . as long as I had you, I would possess everything still . . . and there's a selfish extravagant thought for you . . . but now you're to go to sleep . . . please . . . please . . ."

I said this last with some urgency for he had reached out an arm and he intended to kiss me again. If he did, I was lost for I could never resist the temptation of the flame of the phoenix. I knew equally well that I had no business to keep him talking, for he should have been sleeping long since. I evaded his arm and laid my head on the pillow beside his, put my fingers gently against his lips, whispered . . .

"Your kisses are sweeter than wine, Gregory, and far more intoxicating. I like them beyond anything, but O'Brien said you were to go to sleep. You're very tired and so am I . . . and you know O'Brien. I'll call you later and we'll stroll out to the waterfall. I'll tell you I love you . . . that I love you . . . and again that I love you . . . and again . . . but just for now, O'Brien must be obeyed."

I was asleep myself as I said the words, with my head beside his on the pillow and that was how O'Brien found us a few hours later. I remember she said some mighty hard things about the foolishness of love. Then she pushed him over in the bed and made me lie down beside him. She even spread the eiderdown over us both and he did not wake up even at that. I slept very happily in his arms till he woke up and then as I had promised, I took him walking out by the stream.

The storm had gone over and the sky

was swept clean. The tide was murmuring against the rocks far below us with the sound of bees. I remembered the day I had looked through the rainbow glass of the spray and here it was again with all the colours of the spectrum lighting the valley. With Gregory's hand in mine, I saw Cool-na-Grena . . . saw our future together stretched out there before us, and no shadow of parting. There could be no shadow in this lovely place. I knew it with a calm serenity. We would live there happily ever after . . . day after day, year after year, growing old in contentment together, he and I, in the enchanted land of the rainbow glass.

THE END

Other titles in the Ulverscroft Large Print Series:

TO FIGHT THE WILD
Rod Ansell and Rachel Percy

Lost in uncharted Australian bush, Rod Ansell survived by hunting and trapping wild animals, improvising shelter and using all the bushman's skills he knew.

COROMANDEL
Pat Barr

India in the 1830s is a hot, uncomfortable place, where the East India Company still rules. Amelia and her new husband find themselves caught up in the animosities which seethe between the old order and the new.

THE SMALL PARTY
Lillian Beckwith

A frightening journey to safety begins for Ruth and her small party as their island is caught up in the dangers of armed insurrection.

THE WILDERNESS WALK
Sheila Bishop

Stifling unpleasant memories of a misbegotten romance in Cleave with Lord Francis Aubrey, Lavinia goes on holiday there with her sister. The two women are thrust into a romantic intrigue involving none other than Lord Francis.

THE RELUCTANT GUEST
Rosalind Brett

Ann Calvert went to spend a month on a South African farm with Theo Borland and his sister. They both proved to be different from her first idea of them, and there was Storr Peterson — the most disturbing man she had ever met.

ONE ENCHANTED SUMMER
Anne Tedlock Brooks

A tale of mystery and romance and a girl who found both during one enchanted summer.

CLOUD OVER MALVERTON
Nancy Buckingham

Dulcie soon realises that something is seriously wrong at Malverton, and when violence strikes she is horrified to find herself under suspicion of murder.

AFTER THOUGHTS
Max Bygraves

The Cockney entertainer tells stories of his East End childhood, of his RAF days, and his post-war showbusiness successes and friendships with fellow comedians.

MOONLIGHT AND MARCH ROSES
D. Y. Cameron

Lynn's search to trace a missing girl takes her to Spain, where she meets Clive Hendon. While untangling the situation, she untangles her emotions and decides on her own future.

NURSE ALICE IN LOVE
Theresa Charles

Accepting the post of nurse to little Fernie Sherrod, Alice Everton could not guess at the romance, suspense and danger which lay ahead at the Sherrod's isolated estate.

POIROT INVESTIGATES
Agatha Christie

Two things bind these eleven stories together — the brilliance and uncanny skill of the diminutive Belgian detective, and the stupidity of his Watson-like partner, Captain Hastings.

LET LOOSE THE TIGERS
Josephine Cox

Queenie promised to find the long-lost son of the frail, elderly murderess, Hannah Jason. But her enquiries threatened to unlock the cage where crucial secrets had long been held captive.

THE TWILIGHT MAN
Frank Gruber

Jim Rand lives alone in the California desert awaiting death. Into his hermit existence comes a teenage girl who blows both his past and his brief future wide open.

DOG IN THE DARK
Gerald Hammond

Jim Cunningham breeds and trains gun dogs, and his antagonism towards the devotees of show spaniels earns him many enemies. So when one of them is found murdered, the police are on his doorstep within hours.

THE RED KNIGHT
Geoffrey Moxon

When he finds himself a pawn on the chessboard of international espionage with his family in constant danger, Guy Trent becomes embroiled in moves and countermoves which may mean life or death for Western scientists.

TIGER TIGER
Frank Ryan

A young man involved in drugs is found murdered. This is the first event which will draw Detective Inspector Sandy Woodings into a whirlpool of murder and deceit.

CAROLINE MINUSCULE
Andrew Taylor

Caroline Minuscule, a medieval script, is the first clue to the whereabouts of a cache of diamonds. The search becomes a deadly kind of fairy story in which several murders have an other-worldly quality.

LONG CHAIN OF DEATH
Sarah Wolf

During the Second World War four American teenagers from the same town join the Army together. Forty-two years later, the son of one of the soldiers realises that someone is systematically wiping out the families of the four men.

THE LISTERDALE MYSTERY
Agatha Christie

Twelve short stories ranging from the light-hearted to the macabre, diverse mysteries ingeniously and plausibly contrived and convincingly unravelled.

TO BE LOVED
Lynne Collins

Andrew married the woman he had always loved despite the knowledge that Sarah married him for reasons of her own. So much heartache could have been avoided if only he had known how vital it was to be loved.

ACCUSED NURSE
Jane Converse

Paula found herself accused of a crime which could cost her her job, her nurse's reputation, and even the man she loved, unless the truth came to light.

CHATEAU OF FLOWERS
Margaret Rome

Alain, Comte de Treville needed a wife to look after him, and Fleur went into marriage on a business basis only, hoping that eventually he would come to trust and care for her.

CRISS-CROSS
Alan Scholefield

As her ex-husband had succeeded in kidnapping their young daughter once, Jane was determined to take her safely back to England. But all too soon Jane is caught up in a new web of intrigue.

DEAD BY MORNING
Dorothy Simpson

Leo Martindale's body was discovered outside the gates of his ancestral home. Is it, as Inspector Thanet begins to suspect, murder?

A GREAT DELIVERANCE
Elizabeth George

Into the web of old houses and secrets of Keldale Valley comes Scotland Yard Inspector Thomas Lynley and his assistant to solve a particularly savage murder.

'E' IS FOR EVIDENCE
Sue Grafton

Kinsey Millhone was bogged down on a warehouse fire claim. It came as something of a shock when she was accused of being on the take. She'd been set up. Now she had a new client — herself.

A FAMILY OUTING IN AFRICA
Charles Hampton and Janie Hampton

A tale of a young family's journey through Central Africa by bus, train, river boat, lorry, wooden bicyle and foot.

THE PLEASURES OF AGE
Robert Morley

The author, British stage and screen star, now eighty, is enjoying the pleasures of age. He has drawn on his experiences to write this witty, entertaining and informative book.

THE VINEGAR SEED
Maureen Peters

The first book in a trilogy which follows the exploits of two sisters who leave Ireland in 1861 to seek their fortune in England.

A VERY PAROCHIAL MURDER
John Wainwright

A mugging in the genteel seaside town turned to murder when the victim died. Then the body of a young tearaway is washed ashore and Detective Inspector Lyle is determined that a second killing will not go unpunished.

DEATH ON A HOT SUMMER NIGHT
Anne Infante

Micky Douglas is either accident-prone or someone is trying to kill him. He finds himself caught in a desperate race to save his ex-wife and others from a ruthless gang.

HOLD DOWN A SHADOW
Geoffrey Jenkins

Maluti Rider, with the help of four of the world's most wanted men, is determined to destroy the Katse Dam and release a killer flood.

THAT NICE MISS SMITH
Nigel Morland

A reconstruction and reassessment of the trial in 1857 of Madeleine Smith, who was acquitted by a verdict of Not Proven of poisoning her lover, Emile L'Angelier.

SEASONS OF MY LIFE
Hannah Hauxwell and Barry Cockcroft

The story of Hannah Hauxwell's struggle to survive on a desolate farm in the Yorkshire Dales with little money, no electricity and no running water.

TAKING OVER
Shirley Lowe and Angela Ince

A witty insight into what happens when women take over in the boardroom and their husbands take over chores, children and chickenpox.

AFTER MIDNIGHT STORIES, The Fourth Book Of

A collection of sixteen of the best of today's ghost stories, all different in style and approach but all combining to give the reader that special midnight shiver.